THE FAMOUS FIVE: KNIGHTS' TREASURE

THE FAMOUS FIVE are Julian, Dick, George, (Georgina by rights), Anne and Timmy the dog.

A visit to an old, ruined castle sets the Famous Five on the thrilling trail of a fabulous lost treasure. But the Five are not the only ones eager to find it. They have competition – two dangerously clever men who will use any underhand trick to get there first. The Five must use every ounce of their ingenuity if they are to race them – and make the most exciting find of their lives!

Also available from Knight Books:

The Famous Five and the Knights' Treasure

A new adventure of the
characters created by
Enid Blyton, told by Claude
Voilier, translated by
Anthea Bell

Illustrated by Bob Harvey

KNIGHT BOOKS
Hodder and Stoughton

Copyright © Librairie Hachette
1979

First published in France as Les
Cinq et le Trésor de Roquépine

English language translation
copyright © Hodder & Stoughton
Ltd, 1986

Illustrations copyright © Hodder
& Stoughton Ltd. 1986

First published in Great Britain by
Knight Books 1986
Fifth impression 1988

British Library C.I.P.

Voilier, Claude
   The Famous Five and the
   knight's treasure: a new
   adventure of the characters
   created by Enid Blyton
   I. Title   II. Les cinq et le
   trésor de Roquépine. *English*
   843′.914[J]   PZ7

   ISBN 0-340-37841-7

Printed and bound in Great
Britain for Hodder and Stoughton
Paperbacks, a division of Hodder
and Stoughton Ltd., Mill Road,
Dunton Green, Sevenoaks, Kent
TN13 2YA (Editorial Office: 47
Bedford Square, London WC1B
3DP) by Richard Clay Ltd.,
Bungay, Suffolk

CONTENTS

Chapter One

MONKSMOOR CASTLE

George and her cousins Julian, Dick and Anne were bicycling at a leisurely pace along the road leading away from Kirrin Bay and into the country-side. It was a hot day, and the sun was beating down. Timmy, George's dog, who counted as one of the Five, thought it was *too* hot, and didn't want to dash about as usual. So, after begging for a ride, he had jumped up on to the carrier of George's bicycle, and was now sitting with his nose in the air to catch any cool breeze that might be going.

'You know, I don't think it's a bad idea at all that Uncle Quentin decided we'd stay in Kirrin these summer holidays,' said Julian. 'We've had some very interesting holidays in other places, of course – and some fine adventures on Kirrin Island itself! But I know there are spots not so very far away which we've somehow never got round to exploring.'

'Yes, Ju,' his little sister Anne agreed. 'Anyway, I simply love staying at Kirrin Cottage with Aunt Fanny. And Uncle Quentin has been travelling about so much, to all his conferences and things, that it seems a long time since we had quiet holidays at Kirrin.'

Dick looked as if 'quiet holidays' didn't particularly appeal to him, but he didn't say so. After all, the children *did* love Kirrin, where they had come to spend the summer with their cousin George, as usual. George's real name was Georgina, but she always liked to be called George, because she wished so much she had been born a boy. Her father, Uncle Quentin, was a famous scientist and, if he had to go away to a meeting of other scientists when it happened to be the school holidays, he would often take Aunt Fanny and all four children with him – and Timmy too, of course. This year, however, he had an important book to write, and so he had decided that they would all stay at Kirrin Cottage. Aunt Fanny and the children didn't mind a bit.

'There are lots of things to do at Kirrin,' George said to the others as they all cycled along. 'I'm going to bathe and take my boat out every single day! It will be great fun.'

'Yes, and we can always go for an expedition, the same as we're doing today,' said Dick, cheering up.

'What's the castle called?' asked Anne. 'The one

we're going to see, I mean. Julian told me, but I've forgotten.'

'It's called Monksmoor Castle,' George said. 'It dates back to the Middle Ages. My father told me it was a big fortress then. I've been past it once, in the car, but I've never been inside it before.'

'I like looking at old ruins,' said Julian. He was very interested in history, and had got a good report for it at school last term.

'Then this is your chance!' said George, getting off her bicycle. 'Here we are!'

A moment or so later the Five were following a guide who showed parties round Monksmoor Castle. A lot of people had just got out of a tourist coach and were in the same party too.

Anne, who wasn't quite as interested in history as her brothers and her cousin, was only listening to the guide with half an ear – and dear old Timmy wasn't listening at all, but just sniffing all the exciting smells in the air. He was sure there were mice somewhere in these ruins! The older children, however, were fascinated by the story the guide had to tell.

'This castle,' he began, as he led the party through the gateway, 'was built in the reign of Edward I by Sir Hubert de Monksmoor. Sir Hubert was believed to have had a vast fortune – such a fabulously large one that nobody could even guess how much it was worth. In modern money, it would probably have come to millions of pounds.'

An American lady standing beside Anne let out a gasp of amazement. 'Wow!' she said, awestruck. Timmy must have thought she was talking to him, because he barked, 'Bow wow wow!' in reply, like the polite dog he was! The children couldn't help laughing, and so did several other people.

The guide went on with his story: 'As I was saying, Sir Hubert was said to have had a huge fortune, but it wasn't really his own – he was only looking after it. I expect you've heard of the Order of the Templars? It was founded in the Middle Ages, and its members were a kind of religious order of knights. They were famous fighting men, with branches in England, France, Spain and other European countries. They fought in the Crusades, but they would never swear an oath of allegiance to any reigning king, and they had their own headquarters in several countries.'

'The Temple in London gets its name from the Templars,' Julian told the other children in a whisper. He was following every word the guide said with great interest. 'I read *Ivanhoe* at school last term, and there's a lot about Templars in that too – it's a jolly good story.'

'Well, the Templars grew to be very rich and powerful,' the guide continued. 'King Philip the Fair of France thought they were *too* powerful for his liking, and in the year 1307 he decided to confiscate the goods of the Templars in France, and he had their Grand Master arrested. Now at the Temple in Paris, their French headquarters, they kept a fabulous treasure . . .'

The guide paused, and looked at his audience – everyone's eyes had opened wide at the magic word 'treasure'! They were listening with bated breath! Pleased with the success of his story, the guide went on with it:

'Well, the Pope managed to warn the Templars of what King Philip was planning to do, and before they were arrested, the knights just had time to save part of their treasure, by burying it or by sending it away to safe places. And that was how Sir Hubert de Monksmoor came by a chest full of gold plate, jewels and precious stones and gold and silver coins. There were Templars in his family, so they got the treasure out of France and brought it to him in England for safekeeping. Sir Hubert, so they say, was scrupulously honest about the treasure entrusted to him, and hid the chest in a place whose whereabouts only he knew. Sure enough, the Templars were suppressed and the King of France laid hands on all of their goods that he could get – and then Sir Hubert de Monksmoor died very suddenly, still guarding part of the treasure of the Templars. But he took the secret of its hiding place to the grave with him.'

'So where is it now, then?' asked one of the party of tourists. He had a strong, carrying voice. 'Didn't anyone ever find it?'

'No, never,' said the guide. 'Though not for

want of trying! As I'm sure you can imagine, there have been any number of treasure-seekers after it over the centuries.'

The man who had spoken was tall and broad, with a shock of fair hair and a slow, solid look about him. He was going round the castle with another tourist, a dark, thin, lively little man. The small man grinned and dug his friend in the ribs. 'What a stupid question, old fellow!' he said.

'Stupid?' said the other man, but he didn't seem annoyed.

'Yes, and you got a stupid answer, too!'

'Now wait just a minute!' said the guide, over-hearing them, and not very pleased to think he had said something stupid. 'I'll have you know that –'

'No offence meant!' said the dark little man, chuckling. 'I only meant that if by any chance one of the treasure-seekers actually *found* the treasure, he wouldn't have gone round telling everyone, would he?'

The children smiled, amused, as the guide him-self had to agree. He looked taken aback for a moment, and then said, a little grudgingly, 'Well, I suppose you've got a point there, sir!'

The party went on round the castle, with the guide showing them the different rooms. They were all more or less ruined, and after a while, as one ruin looks much like another, the three younger children began to get a little bored. Julian, who was more grown-up and serious-minded, was still listening with great interest, but Dick, George and Anne were getting more fun from looking at the tourists in the party and making whispered remarks about them.

They were particularly intrigued by the contrast between the lively, dark little man and his big, quiet companion.

'The little one is like a monkey,' said Dick. 'And the big one's like a huge great ox or something!'

'Yes, they're a funny couple,' George agreed. 'The dark one's a real clown, isn't he? Oh, look – he must have had a sugar lump in his pocket, and he's giving it to Timmy. That's certainly the way to make friends with dear old Tim!'

She might have added that it was the way to make friends with *her*, too! All of a sudden she liked the man very much – anyone who was nice to Timmy must be all right, she felt.

Anne tugged at Julian's sleeve to attract his attention. 'Ju, couldn't we go now?' she asked. 'I'm getting awfully tired of trudging round these ruins.'

'It won't take much longer, Anne,' said her brother. 'I do want to see the underground passages and dungeons, and they're next.'

'Oh yes, I want to see them too!' said Dick. 'Dungeons are the most interesting bit of any ruin!'

George agreed with the boys, and at that moment the guide asked the whole party to pay attention: 'Ladies and gentlemen, we are now

going down to the underground part of the castle,' he told them. 'There's no electricity down there, so I'll give you all special wax tapers before we start. Would you come this way, please?'

Then, for the first time, the guide spotted Timmy, close on George's heels as usual. As people often did, he thought George, with her short, dark hair and determined manner, was a boy and not a little girl. 'Now then, my lad, please keep your dog on a lead!' he told her. 'Animals aren't allowed here unless they're under control!'

'Oh dear – I do hope you don't mind snakes!' said the little dark man, calmly taking a viper out of his pocket. I'm afraid I couldn't very well put my little pet here on a lead. There's nowhere to tie one where it wouldn't slip straight off him again. He's quite tame, though – watch out, here he comes!'

The American lady jumped with fright. Two other women shrieked in alarm. One brave man raised his walking stick to bring it down and stun the snake – and Dick and George burst out laughing.

'It's only a rubber one!' said Dick.

The tourists felt relieved – but the guide was very angry.

'That's a joke in very bad taste!' he said. 'What an idea! At your age too, sir! Now if it was a lad like this young fellow . . . ' And he pointed to George, who was still laughing.

'Well, for one thing, I'm a girl and not a boy,' she pointed out, tying a piece of string to Timmy's collar; she hadn't got a lead with her. 'And for another, when I want to play practical jokes on people, they're much funnier ones!'

The little dark man pretended to be very sorry for what he had done. He stuffed the rubber snake back in his pocket, wrung his hands in a theatrical sort of way, beat his breast as if he were full of remorse and said, 'I'm terribly sorry, sir, and I won't do it again, I promise!'

He was so funny that nobody minded his silly practical joke – the whole party laughed instead. 'These English are real cute!' the American lady told a friend.

The guide laughed too, but then he said, 'Now, sir, if you'll please stop fooling about!' He went on telling the party about the history of the castle – and then, at last, asked them to follow him down a flight of steps.

Chapter Two

WRITING ON THE WALL

The whole party followed the guide cautiously down the worn, stone steps. Everyone by this time was carrying a lighted wax taper. The stairs led them to a circular underground room. It had a low ceiling and a paved floor. The guide stopped here and waited for all the sightseers to gather in a circle around him. Then he raised his own taper above his head to light the place up.

'We are now in the antechamber leading to all the underground passages and dungeons of the castle,' he told them. 'I'm afraid I can't actually take you into them, for the very good reason that most of them have been walled up because they were dangerous.'

'Dangerous?' muttered George crossly. She was disappointed – she'd been counting on seeing those underground passages!

'Yes, they looked as if they might cave in, young

man – young lady, I *should* say!' George scowled, even though it had been her own idea to tell the guide she was really a girl. 'It would be very risky to go into them, so they were closed, all except that one over there.'

And he pointed to the opening of a passage which was high enough and wide enough for a medium-sized man to walk down it. Everyone crowded to get a better view.

'All except that one!' he repeated. 'The work-men who were restoring the castle used it as a place to keep their tools and building materials for some time, but it's officially forbidden to go down it now. And it's going to be walled up too, sometime soon.'

Julian, Dick and Anne were as disappointed as George. The exciting words 'underground pass-ages' lost half their magic if you couldn't actually go down those passages; it seemed such a shame!

Seeing their downcast faces, the guide added kindly, for their benefit, 'Sorry, but you're not missing anything. I know how you young folk love a secret passage-way – but I can assure you there's nothing very mysterious about our underground passages here!'

'What, not the least little bit of treasure?' said the dark little man, winking one eye.

'Not the least little bit! I'm sure you won't be surprised to hear that the underground part of the castle was searched several times, very thoroughly, before the passages were walled up. Well, let's go back to the light of day, ladies and gentlemen.'

The party had begun climbing the steps again when a mouse suddenly scurried right across Timmy's path. The dog was bringing up the rear with the rest of the Five. When he spotted the mouse, he let out a loud 'Woof!' like a kind of war-cry, and set off after it so suddenly that the string George was using instead of a lead slipped out of her hand.

'Timmy!' the girl cried. 'Where do you think you're going, Tim? Come back here! Timmy!'

But Timmy wasn't listening. He was much more interested in the mouse which was now darting this way and that ahead of him, teasingly out of reach. 'Catch me if you can!' it seemed to be saying as it suddenly hurtled full speed ahead and disappeared down into the dark underground passage. Timmy let out another bark as he disappeared after it.

George shouted again: 'Timmy! Come *here*! You bad dog!' But seeing that for once he wasn't going to take any notice of her, she too started down the passage.

Thanks to the light from the taper, George could just see her way, and the passage itself was not so full of debris as she might have expected.

Far ahead of her, she heard Timmy still barking at his mouse. She quickened her pace.

Surprisingly perhaps, the only people who had noticed George's disappearance were her cousins.

But the four children *had* been bringing up the rear of the party and were a little way behind the others. 'Oh dear!' cried Anne in dismay. 'The guide said that tunnel was dangerous!'

'Don't you worry – George will be back in a moment with Timmy,' Dick told his sister.

But after a while Julian began to feel worried. He was just about to set off in search of his cousin when she reappeared, dragging an unwilling Timmy at the end of his string 'lead'.

'He really lost his head over that mouse!' she told the others, laughing. 'You've no idea what a hard time I had making him come back. He's in a terrible state!'

Nothing else out of the ordinary happened while they were in the castle, and soon the guide had finished showing the party round. The children fetched their bicycles and set off for Kirrin Cottage, Julian, Dick and Anne looking as if they had enjoyed the expedition very much, although Timmy was cross because his mouse had got away – and George was silent, apparently deep in thought.

Aunt Fanny had a delicious tea waiting for them, with cucumber sandwiches, a rich fruit cake, and raspberries and cream for a special treat. The children were hungry for it, too, after their long bicycle ride and all the time they had spent walking round Monksmoor Castle. But George was still very quiet and wrapped up in her thoughts. It wasn't like George, who was usually so lively and talkative, and Aunt Fanny felt quite worried.

'You're not ill, are you, George dear?' she asked. 'Did you get a touch of the sun this afternoon, I wonder?'

'No, I'm quite all right, thanks, Mother,' said George.

When tea was over, Dick asked his cousin, 'What *is* the matter, old girl? You don't seem like yourself at all.'

'Oh, *I'm* all right,' said George. 'I'm just wondering about something, that's all.'

'About what?' asked Julian.

'The underground passage – and something I saw down there.' George told him.

'You *saw* something. in the underground passage?' cried Anne, looking very surprised.

'Yes, I did – well, I suppose I might as well tell you all about it.'

And George told them her story: she had been looking around, she said, as she went down the passage after Timmy. 'As I went along, I held my taper up so that I could see to right and left of me. When I caught up with Timmy he was barking at a hole – I suppose the mouse had just gone down it. I bent over to put the string on his collar again, and as I straightened up I saw a funny set of marks engraved on the stone of the wall just above me.'

'What kind of marks?' asked Julian.

'Well, sort of hieroglyphics, almost like strange

21

writing. They were mysterious signs, anyway. I didn't have time to look very closely, and they had worn rather faint in places. I can't help wondering about them, though. They just might be meant to tell people where the lost treasure is – do you remember what the guide told us about the treasure of the Templars?'

Dick roared with laughter. 'Honestly, George, what a silly idea!' he said. 'You don't think anyone would go leaving such an important clue just where anyone and everyone could get at it, do you?'

'Not anyone and everyone!' George pointed out. 'Once upon a time nobody but the lord of the castle, Sir Hubert himself, would have been allowed to go down underground there.'

'But all the same, George, lots and lots of people *have* been down that passage over the centuries,' Julian pointed out. 'Even if the marks you saw really are to show where the treasure's hidden, they must have been found ages ago!'

George looked gloomy. 'I knew you'd only laugh if I told you what I'd found,' she said. 'But I've got a sort of hunch that there still *may* be something interesting there.'

'You know, Julian, George's hunches often turn out to be right!' Anne gently reminded her big brother.

'Yes, so they do,' the fair-minded Julian agreed. 'And supposing George's picture-writing on the wall really is about the treasure, we can't be one hundred per cent certain that it *has* been decoded already . . .'

'Only about ninety-nine per cent certain!' said Dick.

'Listen, everyone!' said George. 'Why don't we act as if we thought there was still a treasure to find in the castle anyway? Why don't we go looking for it? I mean, it would be fun, as a sort of game to play these holidays, don't you think?'

'Good idea!' said Dick, suddenly getting enthusiastic about George's suggestion. 'I vote for the treasure hunt!'

'So do I!' said Julian and Anne, both at the same moment.

'Right!' said George. 'Well, we have to start somewhere, and I think the first thing to do is go back to that underground passage and copy the picture-writing down.'

'But how can we get into the passage?' asked Julian, frowning. 'We'll never be able to get down there in the daytime, with all the tourists and guides about the place.'

'We could slip away down the steps unnoticed while we were pretending to look round the castle again,' Anne suggested.

'What, all five of us?' said Dick. 'Tricky!'

'Woof!' Timmy agreed.

'All right, then,' said George, 'let's try getting into the underground passage by night. The castle won't be guarded then – it's mostly ruined, so there's nothing to be stolen. We ought to be able to get into it easily enough!'

Anne was a little worried about the idea, and Julian hesitated at first, but in the end he came round to George's way of thinking, and Anne always felt happy to do as Julian did. The children decided to go back to Monksmoor that very evening. It was a fine night, with a full moon, so the opportunity seemed a good one. They equipped themselves with torches, some rope, paper and pencils, got on their bicycles and left Kirrin Cottage quietly. They didn't want Aunt Fanny or Uncle Quentin asking where they were going.

The stars shone in a clear sky, and it was nice and cool now, so the children cycled along the road faster than they had that afternoon, and this time Timmy ran along at George's side.

Quite soon they came round a corner and saw Monksmoor Castle – a great dark shape looming up ahead of them. The four cousins got off their bicycles.

'We're in luck!' said Julian, glancing round. 'Look at that! There's some builders' scaffolding up against that partly ruined wall. I expect they're restoring it to make it safe.'

'Yes, I'd just noticed that myself,' said Dick. 'Good – we can try getting in that way!'

It wasn't difficult. Once they were up on top of the wall they tied their rope to one of the uprights of the scaffolding, and with its help they were able to slip down on the other side with ease. They tied Timmy carefully to the rope and let him down too; he didn't think much of it, but he wouldn't have wanted to stay behind either.

The Five landed in the castle courtyard, and then made their way through the ruins until they reached the underground antechamber off which the passage led. Timmy recognised the place, and set off down the passage of his own accord. He was obviously hoping to find that little mouse again.

George and her cousins followed him. Their footsteps echoed in a funny sort of way. Anne didn't much like it. She was feeling rather scared, and kept close to Julian. Dick brought up the rear. Suddenly, George stopped. The beam of her torch swept over part of the wall, a place which would be about level with a man's face.

'Here it is,' she said. 'Look at that!'

Dick, Julian and Anne craned their necks to see the strange picture-writing on the wall. There were three lines of it.

'Golly – it certainly does look mysterious!' said Julian excitedly. 'Come on, let's copy the signs down.'

'Pass me the sketch-pad, will you, Anne?' said Dick. He had already got a ballpoint pen out of his pocket, and now he quickly set to work to copy down the strange signs engraved on the wall.

'The stone is very worn,' said Anne. 'It's quite

hard to make out what some of those marks actually are.'

'Yes, and that just goes to show they're very, very old,' George told her cousin. 'Something tells me that they *have* got something to do with the treasure of the Templars!'

'And even if they haven't,' said Dick, as he copied them down, 'we can take them as the starting point for our treasure hunt. Even if it's just a game, we ought to play it properly! There, I've finished!'

He looked at his picture with satisfaction, then folded up the piece of paper and put it in his pocket.

'Well, we'd better go home now,' said Julian, sensibly. 'I think we've done pretty well for one night.'

Timmy was disappointed; he hadn't found his mouse, and would have liked to stay a little longer! He made his feelings known with a pathetic 'Woof!'

But George wasn't having any of that!

'No, Timmy – it's bedtime for you,' she told her dog. 'Yes, I know it was thanks to you I saw this picture-writing, and we're all grateful – but there's going to be a lot for us to do when we start the treasure hunt itself tomorrow, and we need a good night's rest. So do you. After all – we may be in for another exciting adventure!'

Chapter Three

MR LONG AND MR SHORT

The Five set to work with enthusiasm next day. First of all, they decided, they must try to find out the origin of that mysterious picture-writing – but they must go carefully, because they didn't want lots of other people joining in their treasure hunt. And most important of all, they must try to find out what it actually *meant*, bearing in mind the lie of the land and the legend of the treasure.

'We've given ourselves quite a job here, if you ask me!' said Julian. The children were just starting out on their bicycles again. This time, they were going to Monkton, the market town near Monksmoor Castle, where they hoped to find some local records about the castle itself. The idea had been Julian's – but now he was beginning to wonder if they were just off on a wild goose chase. 'Pretty silly we'll look if we spend our holidays looking for information about something that never existed, instead of enjoying ourselves by the sea!'

'Oh, don't be a wet blanket, Julian!' said George.

'We may find a clue in the – what did you call them, Ju?' Anne asked. 'Arks or something, you said.'

'Archives!' said Dick. 'Specially the ones that refer to Monksmoor Castle.'

But they were in for a bit of a disappointment. Once they reached Monkton Town Hall, they explained their business to a friendly receptionist, who telephoned someone in another office, and then said they could go up and see the town clerk. He was a nice old man with a moustache, and he was friendly too. But he couldn't help them much.

'You'd be welcome to see the archives if we had any,' he said, 'but I'm afraid we have nothing much at all! Just the usual registers of births, deaths and marriages – nothing about Monksmoor Castle. It's nice to see young people so keen on historical research, and I only wish I could help you. Why don't you try the museum? They just might have some more information there.'

The children thanked him politely, and went back to their bicycles feeling a little downcast. 'No luck so far!' said George. 'Well, we might as well ask in the museum, as he suggested.'

It was a very small museum of local history – there was nothing much of any outside interest, but then it was local history that the Five were after. There was a woman at the desk who gave them a nice smile, and said it would be all right for Timmy to come in with them if they kept him on a lead – luckily George *had* brought his lead with her today! She seemed quite willing to answer the children's questions.

'Yes, we do have a few exhibits from Monksmoor Castle. And we sell a plan of the ruins so that tourists can find their way about it.'

The four cousins cheered up. This was more like it! Julian immediately bought one of the plans the woman had on her desk.

'It's a funny thing,' she said, handing it to him, 'sometimes we don't sell one of these for weeks, and now I've sold two in the same morning! There were two gentlemen in the museum a little while ago who bought one as well. They seemed to be just as interested in Monksmoor as you are!' She chuckled, and added, 'I must say, they were a curious couple and no mistake! A tall, broad, fair-haired man, and a little dark one who kept putting on a comic act the whole time – he unfolded that plan as if he were going to play the accordion with it!'

Once again, the children exchanged glances. From the description the museum attendant had just given them, it wasn't hard to recognise the two tourists who had been going round Monksmoor Castle at the same time as they had – and who had taken such an interest in the treasure of the

Templars too!

'Well, well, well,' murmured George, under her breath. 'So they bought a plan too, did they . . .?'

And she followed her cousins through the turnstile and into the museum, which was almost empty at this time of day.

Unfortunately, the exhibits in the museum didn't tell the children anything that would help them in their search, and the plan they had bought was a great disappointment too. They had expected to see the underground passages marked on it, but they had been left out altogether.

'Bother!' said Dick crossly. 'We've drawn blank again!'

'Well, it's only what we might have expected,' said Julian, as they walked back to the doors of the museum. 'After all, those underground tunnels have been walled up, and the public can't visit them, so there wouldn't really be any point in putting them on the plan.'

'There's still one place left that we could try,' said George, as they were passing the attendant's desk, 'and that's the Monkton public library.'

The museum attendant overheard her, and smiled. 'I shouldn't be surprised if you found those two visitors I had here earlier in the library as well,' she said. 'I heard them speak of going there too. Well, people are certainly taking a lot of interest in our local history just at present!'

Once the children were outside in the bright

sunlight again, they stopped for a moment to discuss their plan of campaign before going on to the library.

'Don't you think it's rather funny those two men are following just the same route as us?' asked George. 'Mr Long and Mr Short, that's how I think of them – one so tall and broad, and the other so small and dark and lively! If you ask me, there's something mysterious about the way they're behaving.'

'You'd see something mysterious anywhere,' Dick told her.

'Perhaps they're after the Templars' treasure, the same as us,' Anne suggested.

Julian smiled kindly at his little sister. 'George's wild imagination is obviously catching!' he said.

'Yes, old George is making a mountain out of a molehill, just as usual, said Dick.

'But there's nothing to prove I'm wrong!' George pointed out. 'Even if Mr Long and Mr Short don't really believe the treasure exists, they may be going on a treasure hunt just for fun, trying to get on the track of it. After all, that's what *we're* doing! Why shouldn't they do the same?'

'It's possible,' Julian admitted.

'And anyway, you must admit they *do* seem to be taking just the same steps as us,' George went on. 'They went to the museum, they bought a plan of Monksmoor Castle, and they mentioned going to the library.'

'Look, all this talking isn't getting us anywhere,' Dick said. 'Never mind about those two tourists – let's go to the library ourselves!'

The library wasn't very far away. And as the children reached it, they almost bumped into 'Mr Long' and 'Mr Short' just coming out.

'Our treasure-seeking rivals!' Julian whispered mockingly into George's ear.

The two tourists had obviously recognised the children too. A broad smile spread over the dark little man's face.

'Hallo, it's our young friends of yesterday!' he said. 'And how are you this fine day? Isn't that dog dead of indigestion yet? He's very fond of sugar, I must say!'

And he patted Timmy, who had gone up to him and was wagging his tail hopefully.

'What's your dog's name?' asked the slower-spoken 'Mr Long'.

'That depends,' said George. 'Sometimes it's Timothy, sometimes it's Timmy, and sometimes I just call him Tim – so as not to wear his name out!'

Mr Short laughed loudly. 'You're quite a joker, young man!' he said. 'Oh, I'm sorry, I forgot – young lady, I mean!'   .

Mr Long smiled too. 'That's an ingenious idea, I must say,' he said. 'Well, nice to see you again, children.'

And the two men went away. The children went into the library, and Julian asked an attendant who was stamping the books that were being taken out if they could see the librarian. The librarian, whose name was Mr Bryant, said he would be pleased to help if he could, and took the Five into his office. He was a kindly, middle-aged man with a nice smile.

'Well, what was it you wanted to know?' he asked the children.

George glanced at her cousins. They realised she was wondering if they should tell the librarian the whole story, and it didn't take long for them to make up their minds – they felt sure Mr Bryant could be trusted with their secret and wouldn't give them away. Taking turns to speak, they told the librarian all about it.

When they had finished, Mr Bryant smiled. 'Hm,' he said. 'So you're interested in the marks engraved on the stone in that underground passage, and you hope that if you can decipher them you'll find the hiding place of the Templars' treasure – whether there's still anything there or not! Have I got that right?'

'Yes, sir,' said Julian. 'We copied down the picture-writing, and we thought that if you knew of anything to help us we might manage to decode it and find out what it means.'

Mr Bryant took the sheet of paper Dick was holding out to him. He was still smiling, but he shook his head.

'I don't like to disappoint you,' he said, 'but I'm

afraid many visitors to the castle have noticed those strange signs already. In fact, the meaning of some of the hieroglyphics has been discovered.'

The children's faces showed how disappointed they were.

'I suppose we might have known it!' Anne sighed.

'However,' Mr Bryant went on, 'that didn't get anyone much further. The discovery of the meaning of the first few signs never led anywhere. Of course,' he added, 'don't forget that no one has ever deciphered the meaning of the *whole* of the picture-writing, or not as far as I know.'

'Mr Bryant, would it be an awful bother for you to tell us what the signs which *have* been deciphered say?' George ventured to ask.

'Not at all!' said helpful Mr Bryant. 'Look . . .'

Julian, Dick, George and Anne gathered eagerly round to look at Dick's sheet of paper, which the librarian spread out on the desk in front of him.

'For a start,' said Mr Bryant, 'there's this circle, showing a section through the underground tunnel where you saw the picture-writing. The straight line through it is thought to mean one must go straight ahead.'

Julian let out a low whistle. George leaned over the desk to see better.

'The second mark shows the same circle, but with the line through it curving to the left,' the librarian went on.

'So I suppose it means you're to turn left!' Dick said excitedly.

'Quite correct. And the third one –'

'Means turn left again!' Anne said. 'And the fourth one means turn right!'

'Well done! And you can easily see what the fifth little picture shows.'

'Yes, a tower,' said George. 'So after you've followed the underground passage, you come to a tower. The sixth picture is easy to interpret too. It's an arrow pointing upwards, and *that* can only mean –'

'Climb the tower!' Julian finished.

'Yes – I see you get the idea,' said Mr Bryant. 'Unfortunately, however, no one knows what the rest of the picture-writing means. The meaning of the eye, that set of little strokes and all the last part of it has never been discovered. Or if it has, then *I* haven't heard about it!'

'Then there's still hope for us!' said George, cheering up.

Mr Bryant smiled kindly at the excited little girl.

'Well, in any case,' he said, giving Dick the picture back, 'if you're thinking of going on with your treasure hunt, there's no need for you to risk stones falling on your heads down in that underground passage. It's known to come out in an ancient tower, some way from the castle, which is still standing, but has nothing at all mysterious about it. It's known locally as 'The Watch-tower'. I can show you where it is on the ordnance survey map – here!'

'And there isn't any treasure in it?' Anne asked.

Mr Bryant laughed. 'Well, all I can tell you is that no one's ever found any!' he said.

They were just going to thank the librarian and say goodbye when it occurred to Dick to ask if anyone else had been in the library lately, asking him what he knew about the treasure. Mr Bryant said they hadn't – but when the children asked the library assistant, *he* said yes. Two men had been into the library that very morning, he told the children, saying they wanted to look at any books about Monksmoor.

'Mr Long and Mr Short!' said George crossly. 'I knew it! We've got competition in our treasure hunt!'

'You can't be sure of that,' said Julian. 'And anyway it's only a game. Having a bit of competition just makes it more exciting!'

'Mr Long and Mr Short haven't got any picture-writing to help them, either,' said Dick. 'At least, I don't suppose they have. We were the only ones who hung around near the opening of the passage yesterday.'

One way and another, the children were more hopeful than before when they left the library. They thought they might be able to decipher the meaning of the rest of the picture-writing after all.

'And even if it doesn't lead us anywhere, that

won't really matter,' said Anne. 'It will have been fun, won't it?'

After lunch, the Five went back to their treasure seeking. At least they knew a little more now, and they agreed with Mr Bryant that it wasn't any use going back to the underground passage. Instead, they mounted their bicycles and rode off to the Watch-tower.

This turned out to be a sturdy round tower with battlements on top of it, looking very like the picture on the wall in Monksmoor Castle. George was thrilled.

'It must be as old as the castle itself!' she said.

'Yes, I expect it is,' Julian agreed. 'But it looks as if it's been repaired or even restored over the centuries. Come on, let's go round the outside of it first.'

However, a walk all round the tower told the Five nothing new. It was obviously time to go inside and try to discover its secret!

Chapter Four

THE WATCH-TOWER

There was a spiral staircase leading to the top of the tower – the arrow at the end of the last line of picture-writing almost certainly referred to it, and meant that you were to go up the stairs. The stone steps were very worn, and some of them had loose bits coming away from them, but they seemed safe enough to climb.

While she climbed up, Anne couldn't help thinking of the eye that was shown in the picture-writing. None of the children had any idea what it might mean. Anne thought it was rather creepy – she felt as if that mysterious, invisible eye were somehow looking at *her*. The little girl felt a bit scared.

As for Julian, Dick and George, they were thinking of the eye too, though the thought of it didn't scare them. As they climbed the staircase they kept looking to right and left of them, to see if it was by any chance marked on the stone wall of the tower too. But there was no sign of it.

Timmy wasn't thinking of any such thing as he raced up the stairs! He loved to stretch his legs, and this fascinating spiral staircase was just the thing for a dog in need of exercise.

At last, perspiring from their climb in such hot weather, the children came out at the top of the tower. They found themselves on a circular platform with a parapet round it – quite a high one, to keep anyone from falling over, or perhaps to protect the platform. It too was circular, and had a dozen narrow loopholes in it at regular intervals. The top of the parapet looked like battlements; Julian told the others that the proper word for it was 'crenellated'. Up there on top of the tower, they could look out at the surrounding countryside either through the loopholes or through the larger spaces between the crenellations.

The children searched the whole of the top of the tower – and found nothing of any interest at all. Julian said what everyone was feeling. 'Well, there it is! This is the tower all right – but we know no more than we did before.'

'We're not the first to try finding out what the picture-writing means when it points the way to the top of the Watch-tower,' Anne reminded her brother, thinking of what the librarian had told them.

'Oh, don't be so feeble, you two!' said George,

who wasn't giving up hope yet. 'You're not admitting yourselves beaten as easily as that, are you? Don't forget all the mysteries we've faced before – and we've always managed to solve them in the end! So why not this time too?'

'Well said, George!' cried Dick, backing her up. 'After all, we've only been here ten minutes! We'd better search again.'

So the Five went on searching – yes, all five of them including Timmy, who didn't know what they were searching *for*, but was ready to do his duty and join in. They tapped the stones, examined the loopholes, even read the words other visitors had scratched on the battlements, but there wasn't anything which seemed in the least bit interesting.

'I'm afraid there just isn't anything to find,' Dick said at last with a sigh. 'Too bad!'

George flared up. 'Now *you're* thinking the same way as Julian and Anne!' she told him. 'There you are, all three of you, ready to give up just because we're stuck for the moment!'

'We're not ready to give up,' Julian protested. 'However, as searching this tower hasn't led anywhere, perhaps we'd do better to concentrate on the picture-writing itself, if we hope to get any further.'

'What I think –' George began. But the others never found out what she thought, because she stopped short. They could all hear footsteps coming up the spiral staircase. And then George saw Timmy, nose pointing to the top step, begin to wag his tail happily.

'Well, well,' George murmured to herself. 'I bet it's them again!'

And as she spoke, two men appeared at the top of the staircase – Mr Long and Mr Short!

'Hallo!' they exclaimed, when they saw the children. 'Fancy meeting you again!'

Secretly, the children were feeling rather cross. They wished the two tourists were anywhere but here! Timmy, though, barked happily in a very welcoming way.

Mr Short produced yet another sugar lump, making his usual funny faces and gestures as he got it out of his pocket.

'Who's for a lump of sugar, then?' he said coaxingly. 'Is it for a nice doggie – or is it for his missus there?' he added, teasing George.

George could have hit him! But her cousins couldn't help laughing at Mr Short's comical expression.

'Well, children?' said the quieter Mr Long. 'Admiring the view?'

'We've finished admiring it,' George snapped. 'It's all yours now!' And she started down the stairs, with Timmy on her heels and Dick, Julian and Anne after her. The well of the staircase amplified sounds, and they could hear Mr Short up above them, saying to his friend, 'A bad-

tempered little girl, that!'

George went fiery red, but she didn't say anything, and went on down the stairs. When the Five reached the bottom and came out of the tower, they instinctively glanced up. There were the two men, leaning over the battlements and watching them leave. Even though they were quite a long way off, the children could see that they weren't smiling any more. The expression on their faces was rather forbidding.

It was quite late in the afternoon when the Five got back to Kirrin Cottage, and they were feeling more than ready for another of Aunt Fanny's delicious teas. There were shrimps with brown bread and butter today, and iced cherry buns. They played games afterwards, feeling they needed a rest from trying to solve the mystery of the picture-writing. And later that evening when it was getting dark and the moon was beginning to shine, they went down to the beach for a game of ball.

They all had a lovely time, running about on the firm sand, jumping and kicking and throwing the ball. Anne had a very good aim, and even Timmy joined in, getting in everyone's way – not that that bothered *him*. It was a good way for them all to relax after their hard day's work. When they were quite out of breath, they sat down on the beach and listened to the murmuring of the waves.

'Well, now – time we got back to our mystery!' said George briskly. 'We've had a chance to let off steam, so I think this is the moment to put our minds to the puzzle again.'

'All right,' said Dick, taking his piece of paper out of his pocket. 'Well, we know the meaning of that first line – and so do a lot of other people!' he added, sighing. 'But that picture of an eye is still the stumbling block.'

'Perhaps it's meant to be the evil eye, putting a curse on anyone who finds the treasure!' said Anne, shivering slightly.

Julian laughed in a reassuring sort of way. 'I'm willing to take the risk!' he told her.

'If those men don't get to it first,' said George, frowning. 'I'm sure they must somehow have discovered the picture-writing too. And I'm sure that's why we met them on top of the Watch-tower.'

'In which case they're at just the same stage in trying to solve the puzzle as we are,' said Dick, 'so we've got to get one step ahead of them.'

'If you ask me,' said Julian, 'that eye might not mean anything more than "Keep a good look-out!" or something similar. Just to attract your attention.'

'Attract it to what?' asked Anne.

'The next picture . . . all those little strokes.'

'There are twelve of them,' said Anne. 'One of them's got another stroke across it, too.'

'I suppose that means it's been crossed out,' said Dick. 'So there are really eleven strokes in all.'

George thought about it, frowning slightly.

'I'm not sure you're right about that, Dick,' she said. 'If whoever engraved those strokes just wanted to cross one out, wouldn't he have crossed out the last one?'

'Yes, I suppose that *is* the natural thing to do. So those little strokes –'

'And we can't be sure they're so little, either,' George interrupted. 'We don't know what scale they're on, and they could stand for all sorts of things.'

'Sticks?' Anne suggested.

'No, that's not likely,' said Dick decidedly. 'Wooden sticks wouldn't be solid enough or last long enough to protect a treasure.'

'Well, trees then,' said Anne, trying again.

'But there aren't any branches – not in the picture-writing, anyway.'

Anne was determined to contribute to solving this mystery if she could! 'Factory chimneys!' she suggested.

'Oh, honestly, Anne! Don't be so silly!' said Dick, laughing. 'Factory chimneys in the time of Edward I?'

'Wait a moment,' said George, who was still thinking. 'There are twelve strokes, aren't there? Well, up there on top of the tower I noticed that the wall which forms a parapet –'

'Has twelve narrow loopholes in it?' cried Julian, finishing her sentence for her. 'I noticed that too,

George!'

'And *that*,' said George, 'may mean that those twelve strokes correspond to the twelve thin openings in the battlements!'

'Well done!' said Dick enthusiastically. 'Good thinking, George! We must go back there at once!'

'That won't get us anywhere if we haven't deciphered the whole mysterious message first,' Julian pointed out.

'You're right,' Dick admitted. 'Here, let's have another look at it.'

He bent over the piece of paper again. Luckily the moonlight was bright enough for the children to see the copy of the picture-writing quite clearly.

'Well, there's no mistaking *this* picture, or what it means!' he said triumphantly.

George grinned at her cousin. 'My word, Dick, you *must* be brilliant!' she said teasingly. 'I can see the picture shows half of the sun, of course, but that doesn't cast much light on anything – sorry, Dick, no double meaning intended! I mean, how can you tell if it's the rising sun or the setting sun, just by looking at that picture?'

'Oh, I hadn't thought of that,' said Dick, disappointed. 'You're right – we'd need to know. And what exactly is its connection with the strokes – or the loopholes?'

While Julian, Dick and George were trying to work it out, Anne suddenly spoke up in her quiet little voice.

'An eye, and those strokes, and half of the sun . . . couldn't it mean you have to look through the loopholes to see the sun rising or setting, whichever it is?'

And this time she really had made a good contribution towards solving the mystery – or so Julian thought, anyway.

'That's not a bad idea,' he said. 'In fact it's a very *good* idea. But I don't see just what it leads to . . . look, let's sum up, shall we? If the writing is really telling us to look through those slits so as to see half the sun, we still have to find out whether it means the rising or the setting sun. And which loophole are we supposed to look through? Well, we can find that out on the spot, of course, if we go up the tower again.'

'Yes, Ju, why don't we?' said George. 'Let's go back to the Watch-tower first thing tomorrow – just before sunrise! What do the rest of you think?'

'I agree with George!' said Dick, and so did the other two.

'Then that's settled!' said their cousin. 'Now, how about one more game with the ball? And then I suppose we'd better go in and get some sleep – who knows what adventures we may have tomorrow?'

Chapter Five

THE SUN GIVES A CLUE

First thing next morning the Five set off again. The sun hadn't risen yet, and the air was a little chilly.

'Come on, let's hurry!' said Dick. 'We don't want to miss the rising of the sun – though I don't suppose we'll see the running of any deer!' And he broke into a loud and cheerful rendering of *The Holly and the Ivy*.

'Honestly,' said George, 'fancy singing a Christmas carol in the summer holidays, Dick! You're mad!'

'Well, it's a good tune,' said Dick.

It didn't take them very long to get to the tower again. They were feeling very excited as they approached it – would they make a discovery casting new light on the whole mystery once they reached its top?

They didn't take long to climb the spiral staircase either. Just as they came out on the platform surrounded by the crenellated wall, the first rays of the sun were coming up over the horizon.

'Quick!' said George, dashing to the most easterly facing of the loopholes.

The children stood in a line with the smallest at the front so that they could all see over the countryside – they strained their eyes, because they didn't want to miss anything at all. Even Timmy stood on his back legs and got his nose up to the loophole, just below Anne's head! They would have looked very funny like that in a photograph, if there had been anyone there to take one. However, the children were alone, and very glad to be alone too.

Just at that moment, the sun really was looking like the picture that had been engraved on the wall of the passage. It was very bright as it rose, and the children could only squint at it – they knew that you must never look straight at the sun with your naked eye.

'Well, so much for that,' said Dick, slightly disappointed, as the sun rose fully into the sky.

'Yes – I'm afraid I don't see anything special at the spot where it rose,' Julian agreed. 'And the horizon's flat as a pancake over to the east.'

'If we looked to the west, at sunset,' said George, 'we'd see the sun going down over the sea.'

'What use would that be?' asked Dick.

'How do we know until we look?' said George, reasonably enough. 'I suggest we come back this evening, just before the setting of the sun – and the running of the deer, if you like, Dick!'

The others couldn't help laughing, and Dick cheered up a bit.

'Meanwhile, let's take a good close look at all these loopholes,' said Julian. 'You never know – we may have more luck than yesterday, and find some clue in them after all. There may be *some* detail we missed seeing before.'

So they set to work again, patiently inspecting the loopholes. All of a sudden Dick let out an exclamation.

'Come here, everyone – look at this!'

The other three children hurried over to him. Dick was standing by one of the loopholes. He showed them some remains of mortar, obviously very old, still clinging to the inside of the narrow opening.

'Look at these bits of cement –' he began.

'It isn't actually cement, Dick; it's a coarse kind of mortar,' said Julian, scratching the hard substance with his fingernails.

'All right, mortar, if you like,' said Dick impatiently. 'Anyway, it isn't recent. And that seems to prove –'

'That the loophole was once walled up!' George said excitedly, finishing his sentence for him. 'You're right, Dick – well done! Now I see!'

'What is there to see?' asked Anne.

'It must mean that this loophole, the one which was walled up, corresponds to the crossed-out stroke in the picture-writing,' Julian explained.

'And then, later on, the loophole was opened up again – it could have been several centuries afterwards,' said Dick.

'It looks west,' George said thoughtfully. 'Where the sun sets. So that explains it! If we want to find another clue to the hiding place of the treasure, the picture-writing tells us to watch the setting sun through this west-facing loophole. And to do that, it was saying to the people who might go looking in the old days, all they had to do was break the mortar in the loophole.'

But Julian was still working a few things out in his mind.

'I wonder why it's the eighth stroke which is crossed out?' he said. 'After all, this is a round tower, it's no good counting loopholes from one end to another – there isn't an end! Any of the twelve loopholes could be the twelfth. It just depends where you start counting.'

'Perhaps they simply crossed out one of the strokes at random, to show that there *was* a particularly important one?' suggested Dick.

George shook her head. She was beginning to think there was something a bit cleverer behind it all. After a moment or so, she put her ideas into words.

'Listen,' she said, 'suppose the openings correspond to the twelve months of the year? I mean, the sun doesn't rise and set in exactly the same place all the year round. The picture may show the walled-up loophole and tell us, at the same time, that you have to look at the setting sun through it in the eighth month of the year.'

Julian uttered an exclamation. 'Good thinking, George – jolly good thinking! I bet you're right. That explains it all! And the eighth month of the year . . .'

'Is the month of August, and this is August now! I say, aren't we in luck!' said Dick.

'Oh, good!' said Anne, jumping for joy. 'You mean all we have to do is come back this evening, and then we'll know where to look?'

'There's still something bothering me a bit, though,' said Dick. 'The loophole giving the right view over the countryside *has* been opened up again. And that may mean somebody else has worked all this out before us – and if they haven't found the treasure, they may at least have found a clue leading to it.'

'On the other hand,' said George, looking on the bright side, 'it may just be that the builders knocked the mortar out of the loophole when they were restoring this tower.'

'And don't forget ours probably isn't a real treasure hunt,' Julian pointed out, sensible as ever. 'We said it would be fun even if there wasn't any treasure at the end of it, remember?'

'I can't wait for this evening!' said George.

She had to, however, and the day seemed a long

one. But it was still beautiful, fine weather, and so they took George's boat out to Kirrin Island and had a lovely picnic there. Aunt Fanny had packed them up a basket full of good things to eat – pork pies, and tomatoes, and a big bag of fruit, with ginger beer to drink. They bathed, and played games on the little beach in the cove where they moored the boat. But they were keeping an eye on the time, and made sure they got back to Kirrin Cottage quite early for tea. They had already told Aunt Fanny that they were going out after tea, taking the remains of their lunchtime picnic with them, and so they wouldn't need any supper that evening.

'It's such fine weather that we want to make the most of it,' Julian explained, 'so I don't expect we'll be back till after dark.'

Aunt Fanny and Uncle Quentin didn't mind the three younger children being out so late if they had Julian to keep an eye on them – they knew he was a very sensible boy, and grown-up for his age.

The children had already tied the boat up securely to its moorings at the end of the garden of Kirrin Cottage, and now they got on their bicycles and set off for the Watch-tower again. Timmy had done so much chasing about after rabbits on Kirrin Island that he was feeling a bit tired, so he was given a ride on his little mistress's carrier.

The Five were very anxious to watch the sun setting from the top of the tower, so they got there

in good time. The sun was already sinking low in a cloudless sky, and as it approached the horizon the children all clustered around the loophole looking west. Their hearts were thumping with excitement. What would they see? What would they find out? Would they be able to tell what the all-important clue was when they saw it – always supposing it really existed?

The sun touched the horizon and began to go down into the sea beyond the fields that lay between the tower and the sea-shore. The Five were holding their breath and straining their eyes. Down the sun went a little farther. They could only see half of its big red disk now.

'Oh, look!' cried Anne.

'Oh, look!' cried her brothers and George at almost the same moment.

For they had all seen the outline of a farmhouse with a little tower to one side of its buildings, standing out against the sun. It had been there all the time, of course, but they only really noticed it now, looking as it did like a shape drawn in black Indian ink on the red disk.

'Why!' said Julian. 'The shape of that farmhouse is almost exactly like the shape in the picture-writing on the wall in the underground passage!'

'You're right – it's the spitting image of it,' Dick agreed.

George was jubilant. Catching Timmy by his

front paws, she started to dance a jig with him.

'We've found the treasure, we've found the treasure, we've found the treasure!' she chanted.

'Woof, woof, woof!' Timmy barked happily.

The two of them did look a funny sight! Julian, Dick and Anne burst out laughing.

'We haven't actually got our hands on any treasure yet, you know!' Julian pointed out.

'No,' said Dick. 'We'd better go and take a look at the farmhouse, and then we should be able to make sense of the last part of the picture-message.'

'I know that farmhouse,' George told her cousins. 'It's called Monksmoor Farm. When I was little, Mother sometimes took me there when she went to buy fresh cream. The farm used to be part of the estate belonging to Monksmoor Castle, as you can tell from the name. It's changed hands several times, and now it belongs to a farmer called Mr Lofting, who lives there with his family. Actually, I know his daughter Veronica – she's not a bad sort. She's about your age, Julian.'

'Oh, I remember her – we met her once at a party in Kirrin, didn't we?' said Anne. 'I liked her very much!'

The Five went down the spiral staircase of the tower again and mounted their bicycles. It was a beautiful, warm evening, and they stopped on the way to sit in a meadow and eat what was left of their lunchtime picnic. They were back at Kirrin Cottage just as it became really dark.

George was thrilled with the discovery they had made – but she noticed that the boys seemed rather thoughtful. 'What's the matter with you two?' she asked as they put their bicycles away and walked up the garden path.

'Well – the signs seem to be leading us to that farmhouse all right,' said Julian. 'But what could there be that's mysterious about that place?'

'It's got people living in it, you see, George,' said Dick. 'If it was a deserted, tumbledown, old place we could hope to find something there. But what can we expect in a perfectly ordinary, working farm?'

'Oh – all *sorts* of things!' said George, who wasn't going to let the boys damp her high spirits. 'Don't forget, the farm once belonged to the owners of Monksmoor Castle! I shouldn't be surprised if it has lots of surprises in store for us . . . no, I really shouldn't be a *bit* surprised!'

Chapter Six

THE FARMHOUSE

When the children got up next morning, they realised that even though the remains of the picnic had been very good, specially when eaten in the twilight in a country meadow, the exercise and excitement of the night before had made them quite hungry for their breakfast. And it was a good one too, with plenty of eggs and bacon.

'Nobody in the world cooks such splendid breakfasts as Aunt Fanny!' said Julian, finishing off his plateful and helping himself to a nice, warm, brown roll with honey.

After breakfast, the children went out into the garden of Kirrin Cottage. 'Now then, what about that farmhouse?' said Dick. 'What's our next step? We need to get inside it somehow.'

'Nothing easier!' said George, smiling. 'We can go and have tea there this afternoon – Mrs Lofting serves cream teas to tourists in the holiday season.

The family has to make money in any way it can. Veronica once told me her father had to borrow a large sum to modernise the farm and get his dairy herd of Jersey cows going. They're beautiful cows, Anne, with lovely creamy-brown coats – you'll like them! Anyway, the Loftings all work very hard so that they can pay back the borrowed money as soon as possible. And Mrs Lofting's cream teas are quite famous, and *very* good!'

'So we can go and have tea – and keep our eyes and ears well open while we're at the farmhouse!' said Anne. 'I see. I wish we needn't wait till this afternoon, though.'

'I'm afraid we must,' said George. 'I've told my mother we'll go and do some shopping in Kirrin for her this morning. And anyway, I think we ought to have another look at the rest of the picture-writing before we go to Monksmoor Farm, and see if we can make any more sense of it now.'

'Good idea,' said Julian. 'Well, off we go to Kirrin first, then!'

Aunt Fanny gave the children a shopping list, and they got on their bicycles and pedalled off to Kirrin village. It was market-day in Kirrin, with several colourful stalls standing in the main street. The stalls were piled high with vegetables, fruit, flowers, and poultry. There were quite a lot of shoppers – Kirrin was such a pretty place that a good many tourists came to stay there in the holiday season, and they liked to eat the local produce.

Suddenly, George caught sight of Veronica Lofting behind a stall selling butter, eggs and cream cheese.

'Oh, look – that's Veronica, and her brother Terence is with her!' George told her cousins. 'They're selling their mother's things. We'll buy the eggs Aunt Fanny wants from them, and we can say we'd like to have one of Mrs Lofting's cream teas this afternoon. That'll be a good way of broaching the subject of the farmhouse!'

Veronica was a pretty, fair-haired girl, and her big brother Terence looked very nice too. He was a boy of about fifteen, with lively, intelligent, bright eyes.

'Hallo, George!' he said, smiling. 'These are your cousins, aren't they? Julian, Dick and Anne – I think we've met before. And I certainly know *you*, Timmy, old chap! Shake a paw!'

The children bought eggs and some butter from Veronica, and then Dick mentioned that they'd like to come to the farm later that day for one of Mrs Lofting's famous cream teas.

'Yes, do!' said Veronica. 'I happen to know Mum is baking a whole batch of cakes this morn-ing – that's why Terence and I are looking after the stall for her. So it should be a specially good tea today! And we'll be back by then too – we've already sold more than Mum expected! So we'll have a chance to talk to you. That will be nice.'

The children took their shopping back to Kirrin

Cottage, helped Aunt Fanny to put it away, and then went for a bathe in the sea. After lunch, they got out Dick's copy of the picture-writing and pored over it once more, trying to see if they could decipher the end of it.

'After the building, which is just the shape of Monksmoor Farmhouse, there's an arrow pointing downwards,' said Julian thoughtfully.

'Oh, it must mean a cellar!' said Anne excitedly. 'The arrow means we have to go down some steps, and at the bottom we'll find –'

'At the bottom we'll find sacks of potatoes, and bins of feed for Mr Lofting's chickens, and whatever else he keeps in his farmhouse cellar!' said Dick, laughing. 'If that treasure really was down in the cellar, it would have been discovered ages ago, Anne – you little silly!'

'And it *may* have been down there,' Julian pointed out, 'and it *may* have been discovered ages ago! Don't forget, we're probably only playing a game.'

'I'm not as silly as you think, either, Dick,' said Anne, rather nettled. 'I didn't mean I expected to see a treasure just lying on the cellar floor! I was thinking it might have been buried underneath.'

George regretfully shook her head. 'I don't think we'd find it there, either,' she said. 'Anything under a cellar floor would probably have been discovered by now as well.' She thought for a moment, and then went on, 'But I also think that if someone had found the treasure of the Templars at Monksmoor Farm long ago, there'd be a story or legend about it.'

'Yes,' said Julian. 'That guide at the Castle would have told us about it.'

'And if it had been discovered more recently, then the discovery would be well known too,' George went on. 'Somehow or other the news would have got out, even if the finders tried to keep it quiet – it's not easy to hide a sudden fortune, specially in the form of old gold plate and coins.'

'I agree, George,' said Julian, 'And all that rather makes me think that the treasure may still be wherever Sir Hubert de Monksmoor hid it, after all.'

'So it's well worth carrying on with our treasure hunt!' said George.

The Five could hardly wait till it was time to set off for Monksmoor Farm and Mrs Lofting's cream tea. They arrived very punctually at four o'clock, when they knew the farmer's wife usually began serving teas. She was pleased to see the children; Veronica and Terence had told her they would be coming, and she had laid a table for four out-of-doors in the pretty garden of the farmhouse. She soon came out with a big pot of tea, freshly made scones, strawberries and clotted cream, a plate of bread and butter, a jar of honey from the Loftings' own bees, a beautiful chocolate cake and some home-made biscuits.

'I say, this looks good!' said Dick, beginning to tuck in.

The children asked Terence and Veronica to join them, and Mrs Lofting said that was all right. So as they feasted the six young people talked away nineteen to the dozen. George hadn't seen Veronica since last holidays, because Veronica went to a day school in Monkton and George went to boarding school, so the two of them had quite a lot of news to exchange.

'I say, George, did you know we're going to have lodgers at the farm this summer?' said Veronica. 'Actually, Dad didn't very much want to take them, did he, Terry? He was afraid it would make an awful lot of work for Mum, when she already does the cream teas for tourists.'

Terence nodded. 'He said yes in the end, though,' he told the Five. 'We had a very bad harvest last year, and Dad's had to borrow a good deal of money to modernise the dairy, so things are a bit tight here at the moment. Not that that's anything to be ashamed of! Dad and Mum both work very hard to pay the money back, and Veronica and I lend a hand when we can.'

'Yes, I wouldn't have mentioned the lodgers except that you might be surprised to see them here,' said Veronica. 'They're actually arriving today.'

'Are they nice? Have they got any children?' asked Anne, who was always ready to make new friends.

Veronica smiled at her. 'It isn't a family, Anne,' she explained. 'Just two gentlemen – friends on holiday together. They say they're very interested in this part of the country. They called here yesterday, and said they'd like to live a real country life for a few weeks, and asked if we could put them up. Dad was going to say no at first but they pressed him so much, and offered him and Mum so much money if they could have full board instead of just bed and breakfast, that in the end Dad agreed.'

A sudden suspicion came into George's mind.

'I say,' she said, 'what do your two lodgers look like?'

'Oh, one's a great big man, with lots of fair hair,' said Veronica. 'He moves and speaks so slowly he seems to be half asleep much of the time. And the other's a funny dark little man who's always fooling around – quite a contrast to his friend!'

'Mr Long and Mr Short!' said George.

'Do you know them?' asked Veronica, surprised.

'Well, not exactly,' Dick told her. 'It's just that we've met them about the place once or twice. George christened them Mr Long and Mr Short, because of the difference in their height!'

Terence laughed. 'The fair-haired man's name is really Edward Foster,' he said, 'and his friend is called Basil Lawson. They're going to arrive this afternoon, they said, or this evening at the latest.'

The four cousins exchanged meaning glances.

However, before any of them could say anything about their adventures, they heard Mrs Lofting call, 'Terry – Veronica! Could you come and give me a hand, please?'

Several other people had just arrived wanting a cream tea, and were sitting down at tables either in the garden or in the 'tearoom' that Mrs Lofting had made out of what was once a big storeroom next to the farmhouse kitchen. She needed her children to help serve the new arrivals. Left on their own, the Five could discuss this new development.

'You know, I'm beginning to think George was right about Mr Long and Mr Short being on the same trail as us,' said Julian thoughtfully. 'We seem to be coming up against them rather too often for mere coincidence.'

'It certainly is funny,' Dick said. 'They must have found the picture-writing in the underground passage, just as we did, and now they're after the treasure of the Templars.'

'And it's more than just a game for *them*,' said George, frowning. 'They seem to be sure the treasure really does exist . . . I'm getting more and more sure of that myself.'

'Oh, do you really think they're after it?' asked Anne, sounding rather worried.

'That's what it looks like,' said George. 'After all, there are lots of good hotels and boarding houses in this part of the country – all of them open at this time of year, and not too expensive. Why do you think they were so keen to come and stay at a farm which *doesn't* usually take lodgers?'

'Easy – because they'd be right on the spot here!' said Dick. 'They've deciphered the picture-writing, and it's led them to Monksmoor Farm. Golly – I do hope they're not going to get to the treasure ahead of us! That would be very hard luck.'

George clenched her fists. 'Whether our treasure hunt's a game, or a real hunt, we want to get there first!' she said firmly. 'And that means playing every trump card we hold.'

'Right,' said Dick. 'Er – what trump cards *do* we hold?'

'Well, for a start, we can get some allies. Veronica and Terence are very nice, and friends of ours already, so let's take them into our confidence. After all, it's very much in their interests for us to find the treasure, if it's really hidden on their father's land. I think it would be what's called treasure-trove – but Mr Lofting would get almost the full value of it. That would help the family out of their financial difficulties all right.'

'Yes, let's tell them,' Dick agreed. 'Good idea. Veronica and Terence will be fine allies, being right on the spot like this!'

'So we tell them the whole story?' George asked, glancing at her cousins.

'Yes,' said Julian decisively.

Veronica and Terence had finished carrying

trays for their mother, and now came hurrying back to the Five. Seeing how serious their friends were looking – even Timmy, who always followed George's example – they said, rather surprised, 'Goodness, what's the matter?'

'Nothing,' said Dick, 'but we've got something important to tell you. Sit down again, would you?'

Dick sounded so solemn that the brother and sister were intrigued, and sat down as he had asked. And when the four cousins had finished telling their tale, it was quite a while before Veronica and Terence could get over their own surprise.

'You mean you think the Templars' treasure which was entrusted to old Sir Hubert for safe-keeping still exists?' said Terence. 'And it's buried somewhere on our land?'

'It certainly might be,' said Julian.

Now it was Veronica's turn to surprise the Five!

'Well, I for one believe you're right,' she said. 'And for a very good reason . . . when Terry and I were very little, our great-grandmother, who was still alive at the time, often told us that *her* grandmother had heard tell of a treasure hidden somewhere in this part of the country, perhaps even on the land which has belonged to our family for a very long time now.'

'So she did!' said Terence. 'Yes, we enjoyed Great-granny's tales, but we didn't really believe them once we got older. We thought she'd just made them up to amuse us.'

'And Mum and Dad don't believe there's any treasure,' said Veronica. 'But I must say, I *do* sometimes have daydreams about it!'

'And now here you four come with what may be partial proof of the legend!' said Terence, amazed. 'Oh, sorry, Timmy – I mean you *five*, of course. But listen – do you really think Foster and Lawson are after the treasure as well?'

'Yes, we do,' said George. 'Perhaps they're only taking it as a kind of game, as we did at first – but more likely, if you ask me, they hope to lay their hands on a hidden fortune. Anyway, now you're in on the secret you're very well placed to keep an eye on what your lodgers do and say! So could you please watch them closely, and let us know anything of interest?'

Veronica and Terence promised the children to help them as much as they possibly could, and then the Five paid for their delicious tea, said goodbye to Mrs Lofting, and set off for home, cycling as fast as they could. The arrival of Mr Long and Mr Short – otherwise known as Mr Foster and Mr Lawson – at Monksmoor Farm made them feel that there was no time to be lost. They must get down to some really serious treasure-hunting now . . .

Chapter Seven

THE WELL – AND A THREAT

The Five had meant to have a council of war and discuss the situation as soon as they got back to Kirrin Cottage, but some friends of Aunt Fanny and Uncle Quentin's had called while they were out, and were staying to supper. The visitors had a couple of children, rather younger than George and her cousins, who had to be entertained – which wasn't at all difficult, with the garden to play in, and the sea where they could swim. However, the Five couldn't talk about their latest discoveries in front of strangers. By the time supper was over, and the visitors had left, all the children were worn out! The mystery of Monksmoor Castle and Monksmoor Farm must wait till the morning.

That didn't stop the children from dreaming of treasure chests brimming over with riches – and they woke in the morning refreshed and full of enthusiasm.

'Well, what are you planning to do today, my dears?' asked Aunt Fanny, smiling at them.

'Have a bathe and go out in my boat, for a start,' said George. She never tired of swimming and boating – how glad she was she lived by the sea-side!

The other three thought her plan sounded a good one – they could talk as freely as they liked once they were out in the boat, where they couldn't be overheard. When they had rowed well away from the shore, Dick shipped his oars and leaned towards the others, looking very much the con-spirator.

'Well, what about the treasure hunt?' he said. 'Anyone been thinking about it overnight?'

'I expect we all have,' said Julian. 'I know *I* have, and what I think is that our rivals are on the right track.'

'Which is both cheering and worrying,' said George, with a sigh. 'Cheering because if Mr Long and Mr Short are following the same route as us, it does look very much as if we *are* on the right track, exactly as Julian says.'

'But why's it worrying?' asked Anne.

'Well – maybe this isn't a very nice thing to think, but I'm wondering whether they just might find the treasure before we do, always supposing there is a treasure, and then decide to keep it for themselves, without even telling the Loftings they've discovered it.'

'Golly!' said Dick. 'Yes, that's worth thinking about.'

'And another thing,' said George. 'The two men are right on the spot now, so they're better placed to find the treasure than we are.'

'All of which says we'd better get a move on!' Julian concluded.

'Yes – we want to get there first,' Dick agreed. 'That arrow pointing downwards shows that we have to start by going down somewhere.'

Anne still rather liked the idea she had had the day before. 'I vote we search the cellars of the farmhouse,' she said. 'There must be places where we can dig – taking up floorboards first if necessary.'

'Anne, any part of those cellars that *can* be dug *will* have been dug over and over again since the time of Edward I!' said Dick.

'But then, where *can* we go down, if not in the cellars?'

'We can always try the cellars for a start, anyway,' said George, siding with Anne. 'I know Veronica and Terence will help us. They're on holiday from school, like us, and it's very much in their family's interest for us to find the treasure. Come on, Dick, get rowing again! We're on our way back to land.'

It was decided that the Five would return to Monksmoor Farm as soon as possible, so they set off after lunch. Terence and Veronica were delighted to see them. They were thrilled by the thought of a treasure hunt.

'Where did you think of starting?' asked Terence.

'Down in the cellars of your house,' said Julian. 'But we ought to ask your father's permission first.'

The children knew Mr Lofting could be trusted, and told him the whole story, in a rather shortened version. The farmer smiled broadly, and then began to laugh. 'I'm sorry, children!' he chuckled, seeing their rather cross faces, 'but what a ridiculous tale! A treasure! Well, I never! Yes, of course you can search the cellars if you like, but leave them tidy, won't you? I've got a lot of farm stuff down there.'

And he went off, still laughing. George was not very pleased. She thought he ought to take them more seriously, and rather wished she hadn't told him about their treasure hunt.

'I hope he won't go and say anything to your lodgers,' she said, looking worried.

'He won't,' Veronica reassured her. 'Dad's not the talkative kind. Come on, let's go down!'

The farmhouse was very old, and had a great many cellars underneath it – under the farm outhouses as well as the house itself. They were all neat and tidy, well aired and well looked after, but full of all sorts of things. The children searched what seemed to be the oldest of the cellars first, but though they went round carefully tapping the floor

and the walls nothing sounded hollow, and they found not even the tiniest little clue to help them.

By the end of the afternoon they had still got nowhere. Terence and Veronica were disappointed; poor Anne was worn out, and Julian, Dick and George were covered with dust. Timmy had been trying to help, and now had a spider's web on the end of his nose which made him sneeze!

'We've drawn blank,' sighed Dick, putting everyone's thoughts into words.

'Do we give up now, then?' Veronica asked.

'Certainly not!' exclaimed George forcefully. 'We never give up. There's an arrow telling us to go down, so go down we will!'

'Yes – but where?'

'Are you sure you've shown us *all* the cellars?' George asked.

'Yes,' said Veronica.

'Is there anything outside the farmhouse that goes down underground?' Julian suddenly wondered. 'A – a pit, or anything like that?'

'Hang on a minute!' said Terence. 'There *is* the old well – it's dry now, and hasn't been used for ages.'

'A well!' cried Dick. 'That sounds hopeful. Come on, everyone!'

At Julian's request, Terence went off to find a good, stout rope and a torch.

'Why a torch?' Anne asked. 'It's still broad daylight.'

'Yes,' Julian told her, 'but you can bet the daylight won't be quite so broad down at the bottom of a well!'

The old well was behind the main farm building. Julian slung the rope round him, made sure the other end of it was securely tied to a tree, and then asked the others to let him slowly down the well by paying out the rope. As the boy went down, he shone his torch on the sides of the well, examining them closely. All at once he uttered an exclamation. He had just seen a mark! It was a white arrow, pointing downwards.

'Eureka!' he shouted up to the others. 'I think I've found something. Let me right down to the bottom, please. I'm on the right track.'

But once Julian got to the bottom, he had a disappointment. He saw several more arrows, and quickly realised that they had been marked with very modern-looking white paint. They had probably been left there by workmen clearing out the well shaft, as a guide of some kind.

All the same, Julian liked to be thorough, so he tapped the bottom and sides of the well with a hammer, just in case. However, he didn't find anything that sounded like a hollow place behind the masonry. It was tiring work, and in the end he came up empty-handed. All the children were feeling rather downcast by now, and the Five went home to Kirrin Cottage in gloomy silence.

However, they felt better after a good night's

rest, and their spirits revived next morning. They set off for the farm once more, hoping to get better results today. They sat in the Loftings' back garden talking to Veronica and Terence.

'We've got to go on searching even more methodically than before!' George told the Loftings firmly. 'After all, it's possible that the future of your father's farm may depend on our sticking to our determination to find this treasure! Nothing venture, nothing win!' she added, rather grandly.

Loud laughter behind her brought her down to earth. She looked round and saw – Mr Long and Mr Short! Of course it was Mr Short who was laughing.

'Well, children? Enjoying your treasure-hunting game, are you? I'm sure it's great fun, but I shouldn't think there's much chance you'll find any *real* treasure, not after all these hundreds of years. And of course, hunting for treasure can sometimes be a *dangerous* game. Don't forget that.'

The four cousins looked at each other. All of a sudden, 'Mr Short's' jollity and good humour seemed artificial. This was the first time he'd ever said anything openly about treasure hunting, too, and he seemed to want to discourage the children. Why, what he said sounded almost like a threat! And there was a look in his eyes which made them feel that he was certainly their enemy.

Even Timmy, who had liked the little man with

the sugar lumps so much, seemed to have changed his mind. He looked as if he were thinking, 'Well, well, well! You're nothing like as nice as I thought you were after all!' But of course all he actually said was 'Woof! Woof!' in a loud, deep tone.

The two men were already going away. Dick clenched his fists.

'Blow!' he said. 'They must have overheard what we were saying.'

'Well, at least we know where we stand with them now,' said George. 'He was threatening us! And did you notice his tone of voice, and the look on his face?'

'So his funny act is all pretence,' said Terence, rather sadly. 'What a pity! I rather liked him at first.'

'Well, as George says, at least we now know that we've got a couple of enemies on our hands,' said Julian. 'This could be a rather tricky situation.'

'Come on, then, let's not waste any more time!' cried Dick, jumping up. 'Back to work, everyone!'

But sad to say, that day was to bring the treasure-seekers two more disappointments. They spent most of it exploring the two main cellars of the farmhouse rather more thoroughly than the day before, but it was just a waste of time. That was the first disappointment. And the second was the result of a cunning move made by Mr Long and Mr Short . . .

When teatime came, the children felt they could

certainly do with another of Mrs Lofting's delicious cream teas, and today the farmer's wife said she wouldn't let them pay. 'I know my two have enjoyed seeing you here,' she said kindly, putting a laden tray down on the garden table, 'and they won't be free to play with you from tomorrow.'

'Why not, Mum?' asked Terence, looking very surprised. 'This is the first *we've* heard of it!'

'Well, dear, your father is sending the two of you to work for the Randalls in the dairy of their farm for the rest of the school holidays. Times are hard for us at the moment, as you know, and I can manage here with just Janet the dairymaid to help me. I'm sure she'll lend a hand with the teas. Our friends the Randalls are short of people to work for them so you'll be helping them out, and helping your father out by earning a bit of money too. Poor man, he's working hard enough for four at the moment!'

'But Dad hasn't said a word to us about it!' said Veronica, astonished.

'No, it was all decided very quickly, dear,' said her mother. 'Goodness knows, you're both a great help to us here, and so you will be to the Randalls too, knowing the ropes of dairy work! I must say, your father wouldn't have thought of sending you off there, but Mr Foster and Mr Lawson put the idea into his head. "Your children will be glad to be bringing in some money, surely?" they said. "And they'll have company, because the Randalls have children about their age." '

Terence and Veronica were more surprised than annoyed by their father's decision. They didn't mind hard work, and the Randalls, another farming family, were friends of theirs. However, when Mrs Lofting had gone off to take an order for tea from some customers, George exploded:

'You see what those two horrible men have been up to?' she said. 'They just want you out of the way! They think we'll have less chance of discovering where the treasure is hidden without your help.'

'It does look rather as if you're right,' said Terence. 'But we'd better remember the treasure may not exist at all!'

'And if it does, I'm sure you Five will manage to find it on your own,' Veronica added.

However, the cousins felt they had suffered a setback. For the next few days they didn't visit Monksmoor Farm so often. Veronica and Terence weren't there — they set off for the Randalls' farm quite early every morning, and didn't come home till late. And though Mr Lofting had said that, of course, the children could explore his farm, they still found nothing. They were beginning to give up hope of solving the mystery of the treasure and the picture-writing.

And then, one evening, something rather strange happened.

Chapter Eight

ANNE'S ACCIDENT

The Five were on their way home from the farm. They had taken to using a little lane which was a short cut to the main road, and went down quite a steep slope. It was rather dark in this lane as evening came on. Anne, who was leading the way, suddenly uttered a cry of alarm. Her bicycle had just come up against something she couldn't see, but which stopped it with a jolt. The little girl flew over the handlebars and landed in a ditch full of stinging nettles.

Her brothers and George were off their own bicycles in a moment, and ran to help her.

'You haven't broken anything, have you, Anne?' asked George anxiously.

'Here,' said Julian. 'Give me your hand and I'll pull you out of that ditch.'

'Poor old Anne! That was a nasty tumble you took,' said Dick.

Anne was a brave little girl, but she couldn't help crying. She had some nasty grazes, and the nettles had stung her badly. But there was worse to come. 'My ankle!' she said, with a groan. 'Oh, my poor ankle!'

Julian bent to look at it, and saw that it was sprained and already swelling up. His little sister couldn't walk on it, and certainly couldn't ride her bicycle. 'Here, you get on the crossbar of my bike,' he told her, 'and I'll give you a ride back to Kirrin Cottage. Aunt Fanny will put cold compresses on your ankle, and you'll soon feel better.'

'And don't worry about your bike,' said Dick. 'I'll see to that. Coming, George?'

But George was not listening to him. She was standing by one of the sturdy bushes that grew at the side of the lane, looking at something, and Timmy was sniffing the ground near the bush.

'What's the matter?' asked Dick, going over.

'This!' said George. 'Look at this.'

Then Dick saw that there was a piece of stout string tied to the bush. It had been broken when Anne ran into it, and a considerable length of string was trailing on the ground.

'And look at that!' George repeated, crossing the road and pointing to another bush, opposite the first one. 'The other end of the string was tied to this one. Don't you see what that means? Somebody tied this string across the lane to bring down the first person who came along.'

'What a stupid sort of practical joke!' said Julian angrily. 'Anne could have hurt herself quite badly.'

George looked at him thoughtfully.

'I don't think it's just an ordinary practical joke,' she said. 'We always take this short cut on our way back from the farm, don't we? Somebody noticed – and tied this string across our path at just the right moment, meaning to get rid of one of us at least.'

Dick stared at George, his jaw dropping.

'You mean Mr Short and Mr Long?'

Everyone was thinking the same thing.

'That's exactly what I mean,' said George. 'They've already got rid of our two allies by making sure Veronica and Terence aren't around. And now I've an idea they're trying to get rid of us too, so that they'll be free to look for the Templars' treasure on their own, with no risk of any competition!'

Julian burst out laughing – though his laughter was rather edgy. 'Oh, honestly, Georgina dear, your imagination's running away with you again! You don't have to go accusing Foster and Lawson straight off, just because someone with a poor sense of humour has stretched a piece of string across a country lane!'

George really hated to be called Georgina, and scowled at her cousin.

'Think whatever you like, then,' she said, shrugging her shoulders. 'I'm sticking to my own opinion. Mind you, I jolly well hope I'm wrong! But something tells me I've got it right!'

Julian started off, with Anne perched on the crossbar of his bicycle, and Dick and George got on their own cycles again.

'Well, *I* think you're right, George,' said Dick gloomily. 'Those two men seemed quite nice at first, but now they look like enemies – and I don't think they make good enemies at all. We'd better be on the watch – they may have some more little surprises in store for us!'

Aunt Fanny exclaimed with alarm when Julian carried his sister into Kirrin Cottage, and hurried to put a cold compress on the little girl's ankle. She said Anne must keep perfectly still. So Anne lay on the sofa like a queen during supper, and had everyone waiting on her!

'You'll feel much better after a good night's sleep, dear,' Aunt Fanny told her. 'However, I think you'd better not walk on that foot for a day or so, and it will be a little longer still before you ought to ride your bicycle again.'

Next day George and Dick kept Anne company while she lay in a deckchair in the garden. Julian went into Kirrin village on his own today to do his aunt's shopping for her.

The boy was feeling rather worried after his sister's accident. He set off for Kirrin on his bicycle. It was market-day again, but the bright, colourful scene didn't seem nearly as much fun when he was on his own. And he couldn't talk to Terence and Veronica today either – they were working on the Randalls' farm. Janet, who helped Mrs Lofting with the dairy, was looking after their stall today.

Julian went over to her to buy eggs and butter. 'Hallo, aren't the others with you?' she asked, in surprise.

Julian told her about Anne's accident, though he didn't pass on George's suspicions.

'Well, what a stupid sort of trick!' said Janet. 'Somebody must have fixed that string up just before you left! I'm sure of that because I happened to see Mr Foster and Mr Lawson coming out of that lane not long before, and they'd have mentioned it if there'd been a piece of string across their path, wouldn't they? They'd have tidied it out of harm's way, too!'

'No, quite the opposite!' Julian was thinking to himself. 'It looks more and more likely that they put it there themselves! So George was right after all!'

He said goodbye to Janet and hurried back to Kirrin Cottage, to tell the others what he had learned.

'I'm not a bit surprised,' said Dick. 'They aren't even bothering to hide what they're up to any more! Do you know what they went and did while you were out shopping? They threw Timmy a poisoned meatball through the garden fence!'

'It's a good thing he's such an intelligent dog,' said George, who was obviously very angry indeed. 'He wasn't going to be tempted to gobble up the meatball – he started barking like mad, and wouldn't touch it. So Dick and I came running, just in time to see those two men disappearing round the corner of the road. And you needn't ask me how I know the meatball was poisoned, because I took it straight to my father, and he only had to cut it open and take one sniff to be sure.'

'What cowards they are!' said Julian indignantly. 'First of all they had a go at poor Anne, and now at Timmy! What else did Uncle Quentin say about that meatball, by the way? Did you tell him about Mr Long and Mr Short?'

'You bet I didn't!' said George. 'I took very good care to keep quiet about them! My father would only want to interfere, and then we couldn't act as free agents any more.'

'All the same, I think we must start to be very, very careful,' said Julian. 'The long and the short of it, if you don't mind my using the expression, is that our friends have shown their hand, and it looks as if they won't stop at anything.'

'Well, *I'm* not stopping for *them*!' said the furious George. 'I'm going to get my own back on them, for Timmy's sake. Though as a matter of fact he's very well able to get his own revenge. They'd better look out!'

She was in such a rage that her cousins had some difficulty in soothing her, but in the end she calmed down.

'Anyway, it looks as if war's declared now,' Dick said. 'We *know* those men are dangerous. We must be on our guard after this.'

Anne was better next day, but she still couldn't move about much. Julian offered to go shopping for Aunt Fanny on his own, as he had done the day before.

'And I'll stay at home to amuse Anne this afternoon,' he told Dick and George. 'Then you two can go out.'

The tall boy swung himself into the saddle of his bicycle, and set off for Kirrin. Aunt Fanny had ordered two nice fresh chickens, and he was going to pick them up. He fetched the chickens, got on his cycle again and was starting to pedal home at a good speed, when a dog suddenly shot out from a hedge, and nearly went under his wheels. Julian swerved instinctively to avoid the animal, putting his brakes on hard.

And then, to his horror, he discovered that the brakes of his bicycle were not working.

Chapter Nine

TROUBLE AT SEA

Before Julian fully realised what was happening, he found himself in the ditch, just as Anne had the day before yesterday.

Luckily he was more shaken than hurt, but he felt very angry when he looked at his bicycle and saw that the brake had been almost completely filed through, so that it would snap as soon as he tried applying it hard. Julian realised that he was the victim not of an accident, but a cold-blooded attack. Why, he might have been killed!

He pushed the bicycle back to Kirrin Cottage, and went to tell the others what had happened to him. He was furious.

'Mr Short and Mr Long again, you can bet!' he said. 'We'd better tell Uncle Quentin about this.'

George began to laugh, though it wasn't very merry laughter.

'And you were telling me *I* let my imagination

run away with me!' she said. 'Well, you're no better, Ju! You say those two men filed through your brake, but you've got no proof, have you?'

'I don't need proof,' said Julian. 'Janet saw the men come out of the lane just before Anne fell off her bicycle. They tried poisoning Timmy yesterday, and they must have sabotaged my bicycle while I was inside the shop fetching the chickens today. I'd left it leaning in a little alleyway near the butcher's, and they saw their chance!'

'But you can't prove it,' George repeated. 'And my father won't be able to do anything without evidence of some kind. The police wouldn't believe him – still less us. No, we'll leave Father to get on with his work, and we won't bother Mother. She'd be terribly worried about us, and I don't want that. I should hope the Five can look after themselves without calling in grown-ups! And as soon as Anne's on her feet again, we'll go back to Monksmoor Farm, and this time we'll jolly well find the treasure!'

Brave words! But Dick was dubious. 'Suppose Mr Long and Mr Short find it first?' he said.

'I've got one of my hunches,' said George firmly, 'and it tells me they won't. Let's trust to our luck!'

She sounded so sure of herself that her cousins cheered up.

That afternoon, Dick and George left Julian playing a game of draughts with Anne and went down to the beach. They thought they'd do some underwater diving. Timmy went with them. He was delighted to have an outing, and jumped happily aboard George's rowing boat. The two cousins rowed hard, and were soon well away from the shore.

'I know a very good place,' said George, pulling strongly on the oars. 'It's quite a way off, but the sea-bed is very attractive when we get there, and there are some lovely fish to watch.'

'Won't it be too deep for us to anchor in that sort of place?' Dick asked.

'No, it's just about right,' George told him. So when they reached the spot, Dick threw out the anchor. Then they got into the diving suits Uncle Quentin had given them. Each suit had a small oxygen supply attached to it, so that the children could swim underwater for quite a long time without needing to come up.

George and her cousins would have hated to go *fishing* underwater — they thought it was cruel, because one might harpoon a fish and wound it instead of killing it. They much preferred to watch the gleaming creatures swimming about. Dick and George swam slowly through the seaweed, made their way around dark rocks, scattered shoals of silvery little fish as they passed by, and watched the sea anemones rippling in colours of pink and purple.

At last they had had enough, and went up to the surface again. Then a cry of amazement rose to the

children's lips – their boat had disappeared! Or not quite disappeared, for they could see it in the distance, being carried out to sea by a fast current.

'I don't believe it!' gasped Dick, taking off his diving mask. 'I *know* I left the boat securely anchored.'

'Timmy!' cried George. 'Dear old Timmy is still on board!'

But he wasn't. A loud barking made her turn her head, and she saw Tim swimming towards her. He wasn't far away – and he was holding part of a coat sleeve in his mouth!

At much the same time, Dick spotted a motor-boat making away from them at high speed, going towards the distant shore. There were two men in it, and although they were too far off for the children to be able to see their faces properly, they guessed at once who they were, and what they had just been doing.

Dick and George were right. Mr Long and Mr Short had been watching the two cousins through fieldglasses, waiting for them to dive. When they did, the men made for the rowing boat and un-hooked the anchor chain – though Timmy was snapping at them the whole time in a most alarm-ing way. Once the boat was drifting with the tide, they went away in their motorboat again, leaving the children to get back to shore by swimming – if they could.

'What a rotten thing to do!' said Dick. 'It won't

be their fault if we don't drown!'

'Timmy obviously did his best to stop them,' said George. 'I just hope he got a mouthful of whatever was under that coat sleeve as well as the sleeve itself! He must have fallen in the water during the struggle, and they left him there while they made off, the brutes! Well, come on, Dick – come on, Timmy. We'll just have to swim for it.'

Both cousins were good swimmers, but luckily they didn't have to swim the *whole* way back. A little fishing boat spotted them, and came to their aid when they were about half-way to the shore. Dick was glad to be on board; he was beginning to feel his strength failing, and even George and Timmy were having some trouble in keeping afloat.

The fishermen, who knew George and her father, were very kind, and went after the rowing boat to retrieve it and tow it home.

'No wonder it was drifting away so fast, Master George,' said the captain of the little vessel – he remembered that George liked to be addressed as a boy! 'Your anchor chain had come unhooked – I never saw a thing like that happen before. Funny, I call it!'

Dick and George exchanged meaning glances. *They* knew the explanation. But yet again they had no real, solid proof that Foster and Lawson were responsible.

That evening the children discussed what had

happened, and decided that they had better keep quiet about this latest 'accident', just as they had kept quiet about Julian's bicycle.

'I don't like this a bit, though,' said poor little Anne, shivering. 'Those men could murder us!'

'No, I don't think that's their idea, Anne,' Julian said, trying to cheer her. 'They're certainly pretty shady characters, but I think they only want to frighten us into giving up our search for the treasure.'

'I agree, Ju,' said Dick. 'Mr Long and Mr Short don't actually want us dead, just out of their way – though they certainly go to some lengths to persuade us to leave them alone!'

Anne's ankle was much better now, and within a day or so she was on her feet again. The Five went back to Monksmoor Farm, where the Loftings were pleased to see them – but their lodgers very obviously weren't. The children had made up their minds they weren't going to let Foster and Lawson, otherwise Mr Long and Mr Short, frighten them, but they were on their guard all the same.

They had settled on a plan of action beforehand. They pretended not to be looking for the treasure any more, and made out they had only come to the farmhouse for one of Mrs Lofting's cream teas. And they didn't have to pretend to be enjoying that! Unfortunately, Mr Long and Mr Short looked as if they had no intention of going away nd leaving the children alone, and if they were around the Five couldn't search properly. Obviously they must think of something.

They were bending over the picture-writing yet again that evening, studying it for about the hundredth time, when Anne said, rather timidly, 'You know, while I was lying with my foot up I kept on thinking about that arrow pointing downwards, and the sign just after it, and I did have an idea.'

'All that sign looks like to me is a worm wriggling along the ground,' said Dick. 'I don't see what *that* could be telling us!'

'Perhaps it's suggesting a snake hunt!' laughed Julian.

'Or a swim in the sea!' added George. 'After all, the wavy line could stand for water.'

'Well, that's exactly what I was thinking,' said Anne earnestly, pointing to the sign which followed the arrow. 'I think it *does* mean water.'

'But there's no water beneath ground level at the farm,' Dick objected.

'Yes, there is,' said Anne. 'In that old cistern!'

Julian, Dick and George looked at each other. Their mouths dropped open!

'The cistern,' George repeated. 'You mean that curious old construction next to the stables in the farmyard?'

'That's right,' said Anne. 'Why not? If we go down, we'll find water in it – so why not the chest of treasure too? I mean, the last picture but one must show the Templars' treasure chest, mustn't it?'

'Anne is right!' said Julian. 'We never thought of the cistern as an underground place to look, just *because* it has water in it, but that wavy line is a real clue! Anne, you're brilliant! Well done. There's something to be said for sprained ankles after all, if they give you brainwaves like that!'

The others enthusiastically congratulated Anne too. And then they settled down to drawing up a new plan of action.

'I don't think we can do this by daylight,' said George. 'If today was anything to go on, our friends Mr Long and Mr Short will stick close. No, we must explore the cistern by night.'

'Hm,' said Julian, doubtfully. 'I don't think Uncle Quentin will give us permission to do that, you know.'

'Then we won't ask him!' said Dick. 'After all, we're not planning to do anything wrong, are we? Quite the opposite! Remember what it will mean to the Loftings if we find the treasure on their farm.'

'It could be dangerous, all the same,' said Anne, sounding a little frightened.

'As I was saying the other day, nothing venture, nothing win!' George told her cousin. Anne thought privately it was all very well for George to talk – *she* wasn't afraid of anything. Lucky George!

'Anyway,' George went on, 'you won't be going down into the cistern, Anne, not with your ankle still a bit shaky. I'm going down there myself, on my own – yes, I am, Ju! It's my turn. You explored the well, I'm going to have a go at the cistern. Right – we're off to Monksmoor Farm this evening, then. What do *you* say, Timmy?'

'Woof! said Timmy, with enthusiasm. 'Woof, *woof*, WOOF!'

And so, that night, once Aunt Fanny and Uncle Quentin were asleep, the Five got out of bed, dressed in dark clothes, put torches and ropes into the saddle-bags of their bicycles, and pedalled off towards what they hoped would be the final stage of their exciting adventure . . . .

Chapter Ten

AN EXCITING EXPEDITION

The Five had no difficulty in getting into the Loftings' farmyard. The farm dogs knew the children and Timmy very well, and didn't even bark. By this time of night, Mr Long and Mr Short should be asleep, like the farmer himself and his family . . . 'So here goes!' murmured Julian, stopping beside the cistern. 'Let's take the cover off it for a start.'

Between them, they lifted the heavy cover off the top of the cistern. Then they leaned over the edge to look down.

'There *is* some water there, but only right at the bottom,' said Anne.

'Yes,' Dick agreed. 'I don't think this cistern's in use at the moment. Well, we'd better go down – oh, good! There are some pieces of iron set into the sides. Look, they make a kind of ladder. But mind how you go, George,' he added, seeing his cousin

,etting ready to climb down. 'They may be rusty. Make sure they'll support you before you put your weight on them.'

'Oh, I'll be all right,' said George. 'I wasn't born yesterday, you know, Dick! I'll put this rope round my waist, as Julian did going down the well the other day. Then I'll feel perfectly safe. Let's tie the other end of the rope to the cistern itself.'

When George was ready, she began her cautious descent. Her cousins leaned over the edge of the old cistern, shining their torches down so that she could see her way. They never took their eyes off her, and Timmy was watching too, looking rather worried.

'It's all right!' George called up. 'These irons are fine – they're good and solid, and well fixed in place.'

Then, all of a sudden, her cousins saw her stop. She switched on her own little torch, which was hanging round her neck, so that she could take a close look at part of the circular wall of the cistern. Something level with her head had caught her eye.

'I say!' she called up, after a moment or so. 'There's an opening here – it's just big enough for a smallish person to climb into it. I wonder if it could possibly be a passage, and if so where does it lead? Hang on a minute! I'm going to find out.'

'George, do be careful!' shouted Julian, leaning even farther over the edge of the cistern.

But even as he spoke, George had disappeared

into the hole in the side of the cistern – all her cousins could see of her was her feet, and then they vanished too. Dick paid out the rope, which began jerking downwards as George went on. Then she stopped. Time passed by – she must be exploring something on the spot. After a while Dick tugged at the rope, and much to his alarm, he felt nothing in the way of resistance. A moment later its dangling end came into sight. George herself had disappeared.

Julian, Dick and Anne looked at each other in dismay. What had become of their cousin? Why had she untied herself? What had happened to her?

'George!' wailed Anne, sobbing.

'I'll go down and look for her,' Julian decided.

And he was just tying the rope firmly round his own middle when a dark head popped up over the side of the cistern.

'Cuckoo!' called George. 'Here I am! Hallo – were you getting worried? Sorry, but that rope was in my way, so I took it off. Golly – if you only knew what I've found!'

'Honestly, George, you really are the limit!' said Julian, quite angrily.

'Oh, look, I really *am* sorry, Julian, but you can tell me off later. Do listen to me now.'

And George told her cousins that the tunnel leading out of the cistern was actually a walled passage, quite easy to get along. It went down to a cave in the cliffs beside the sea.

But what can that have to do with the treasure of the Templars?' Dick wondered. He felt disappointed. 'I suppose the passage was once a secret way out of the Monksmoor estate, and people could escape from the castle along it if an enemy attacked – but a cave's not much good to us. I mean, anyone could get there from the sea, or just be walking along the beach!'

'Yes, you're right there,' George had to agree. 'However, maybe there's a secret hiding place somewhere inside the cave? I'd go so far as to say there *must* be one! If there isn't, why does the picture-writing show it?'

'Does it show it?' asked Anne, puzzled. 'The cave, I mean?'

'Well, not exactly, but almost. I mean, the arrow shows we have to go down the cistern and the wavy line shows water – not the water in the cistern after all, but the waves of the sea, just as I thought before. So the treasure must be somewhere near the sea.'

'You could be right,' said Julian. 'Did you notice just where the cave was, approaching it from the outside?'

'Yes, of course I did,' said George. 'I can bring you all straight there tomorrow, and we won't need to come back here and go down the cistern either!'

The children were tired and excited when they finally got to bed that night. Luckily Aunt Fanny and Uncle Quentin had not heard them come in.

They felt that victory was within their grasp. It *would* be nice to find that treasure, and hand it over to the Loftings . . .

They had rather a short night's sleep, even though they got up later than usual next morning, but they were still eager to set out on the treasure hunt again.

'Let's take the rowing boat round to the treasure cave,' said George.

'Don't call it that yet,' said Julian, cautiously. 'Even if the treasure once *was* there, it's quite likely to have gone by now. Plenty of people have been in that cave before us.'

'Don't be such a wet blanket, Ju!' said his brother. Nothing was going to shake Dick's confidence, not now he had a trail to follow! 'Even if we haven't got all that much chance of really finding a treasure, we still have to *try*!'

A little later they were in the boat, going along the coast towards the cave that George had found the previous night. George and Dick were rowing, while Julian scanned the horizon, and Anne was explaining things to Timmy, who listened to the little girl as if he understood every word.

'You see, Timmy, the sign which comes after the wavy line must be the chest containing the Templars' treasure, and the last one – that straight line – well, I suppose it's just the ground on which the chest full of treasure stands!'

Julian smiled. He only wished they were likely to

find the chest of treasure so easily! Thinking about it, he felt sure that if there was a hiding place in the cave, it must be a very well concealed one.

'Watch out!' George exclaimed. 'We're coming close.'

She pointed to a dark cavern among the rocks by the shore. It was roughly dome-shaped, and opened onto a nice sandy beach.

'By my calculations it'll be a good two hours before high tide,' George went on. 'So that gives us plenty of time to search.'

'And with all of us at work, it will be rotten luck if we don't find *some* kind of clue,' said Dick.

'Woof!' Timmy agreed.

Dick anchored the rowing boat, saying to George, 'I wish we hadn't lost that good anchor and chain out at sea — or rather, I wish Mr Long and Mr Short hadn't lost them for us! This new anchor's all right, but I don't much like using a rope. Couldn't you get a replacement chain?'

'I couldn't find a really good one in Kirrin,' George told him. 'I'll have to go to town some time and buy a new one. Meanwhile we must just make do with the rope. It's a good stout one, though, so don't worry.'

The Five jumped out of the boat on to the firm sand, and went into the cave, switching on their torches. The place was bigger and deeper than it looked from outside. The ground rose in a slight slope, going quite a long way into the heart of the cliff.

'Well, here we are at last!' said Julian. 'Come on, let's set to work.'

In his methodical way, he took charge, giving everyone a different part of the cave to explore. It looked as if it wouldn't be easy to search the place – the sloping ground was all overgrown with slippery seaweed.

George showed her cousins the opening of the tunnel that led out of the cistern at Monksmoor Farm. It was some way above ground level.

'I should think the sea reaches the end of the passage at high tide,' she said. 'It may even get a little way inside. There's a lot of wet seaweed up there, anyway.'

Then they all set to work exploring the cave. Gradually, they made their way further and further in. Anne searched the lower parts of the cave and George and Dick scrutinised it higher up. Julian himself, as the tallest, searched the very top bits. At one point he saw a hopeful-looking crack in the rock, well above even his reach and asked Dick to give him a leg up so that he could inspect it, but it led them nowhere.

Time went by. The four cousins did their best to discover anything in the mysterious cave which might lead them to a hiding place, or another concealed tunnel, but they had no luck at all.

Timmy sniffed the ground too, sometimes scratching at those rocks within his reach, but all he did was dislodge a lot of little yellow crabs from a rock pool.

Suddenly, when the two boys and George were at the very back of the cave, Anne uttered a cry of alarm. She was near the cave entrance, and had just noticed that the water was rising. 'Look – the tide's coming in!' she said. 'Quite fast, too.'

'Oh, blow!' said Dick. 'We forgot to keep an eye on the time – and the tide.'

'Which, as the proverb says, wait for no man!' remarked Julian, rather grimly. He was cross with himself for forgetting to take precautions. 'Come on, let's get home, quick!'

But as soon as the children emerged from the cave they saw an alarming sight. The sky had turned black as ink, and the sea was black too, its large, rough waves topped with white foam. A flash of lightning lit up the sky, and was followed almost immediately by a tremendous thunderclap.

'We ought to have looked at the barometer before we set out!' said Julian. 'What an ass I was not to think of that! And Uncle Quentin counts on me, as the eldest, to be sensible and look after you all!'

Another flash of lightning and another thunderclap interrupted him. At the same moment, a huge wave broke on a nearby rock, drenching poor Julian from head to foot.

The spray hit George, Dick and Anne as well, and next moment heavy rain began to fall. The storm was raging with a vengeance now.

'Come on, let's get back to the boat!' shouted Dick. 'Come *on*, George!'

But George was rooted to the spot with horror, staring at the place where Dick had anchored her boat when they arrived. Because – it wasn't there any more!

'It . . . it's broken its moorings!' stammered Dick, stunned.

'It can't have done!' said George. 'We had the anchor well in place and that was a good stout rope – I wouldn't be a bit surprised if this wasn't Mr Long and Mr Short at work again. They must have been watching our movements from a distance. Oh, I ought to have left Timmy on board to guard the boat!'

'We might not have heard him bark,' Dick pointed out.

'Anyway,' said Julian, 'we can't possibly go home now, either by sea or along the beach. I'm afraid it would be far too dangerous to try swimming in those waves, and the tide's already covered the path along the foot of the cliffs.'

'Then all we can do is go back into the cave and down the underground tunnel,' said George, pulling herself together again.

'That does seem to be the only way,' Dick agreed. 'Which is a pity – because if Mr Long and Mr Short see us coming up from the cistern they'll soon realise that we really are on the trail of the treasure.'

Anne ventured to make a suggestion. 'We might wait in the passage until the tide's gone down again,' she said in a rather scared voice.

'What a rotten idea!' said Dick, crushingly. 'I can just see us shivering there for hours and hours in these wet clothes!'

'Evidently the tunnel's our only chance,' said Julian, who was really very worried. 'In fact, it's high time we started down it. If we stay here the waves may well knock us unconscious, and then we'll be done for!'

So the Five beat a hasty retreat. They were very upset, particularly George and Julian. George was furious at losing her beloved boat, and Julian was angry with himself for his lack of caution. As for Dick and Anne, they were worried about the risk of meeting their enemies as they emerged from the cistern, thus putting them on the right track.

'Hurry up!' shouted Julian, through the roar of the storm. 'Hurry up! The tide's rising faster and faster. We'll only just have time to reach the tunnel – in fact I'm not too sure we *will* reach it, but we must try. It's our only chance!'

And Julian was right to worry. When George had first found the cave, it had been empty and comparatively dry. She had been able to scramble down the slope of its rocky wall, take a look at the beach, and then climb back up again without too much difficulty.

Things were very different today. They had to

haul themselves up to the opening, high in the wall of the cave, by hanging on to wet, slippery stones, and by now the waves were beating against the rocky walls so stormily that the children had difficulty in keeping their footing.

Once they reached the entrance to the passage, Julian and Dick tried giving each other a leg up, but it was no good. Whichever of them was underneath, the waves kept upsetting their balance. In the end they had to give up the attempt to reach the opening.

By now the water in the cave had come up to their chests, and Anne, the smallest, would soon have to swim to keep her head above water. How were they ever to keep afloat in this stormy sea as it filled the cave and rose higher and higher?

'We'll never get out of here!' muttered Dick, dismayed.

'Come on, everyone,' said George. 'Let's go to the very back of the cave, where its floor slopes highest. We can hold out there for some time yet!'

'Yes, and then what?' said Julian gloomily.

'Well, then we'll see!' said brave George. 'First things first!'

Grabbing Timmy, who was struggling to keep afloat, as a wave threatened to sweep him away, she made for the farthest end of the cave, not without difficulty. It was very dark here. Sea water had spoilt the batteries of the children's torches, so they couldn't see anything much.

'There's no way out,' said Dick. 'Perhaps we'd do better to try the sea? If we swam *very* hard –'

'You know that's no good, Dick,' said Julian, who was helping Anne. 'The waves are too fierce for us to have any chance. We'd drown!'

'Come *on*!' called George urgently. She was carrying Timmy now. Soon the Five had reached the very end of the cave, where they were only in the water up to their ankles.

But the tide was still rising . . .

Chapter Eleven

THE END OF THE TREASURE HUNT

Rather desperately, Julian looked around him. 'See that?' he asked suddenly. 'There's a kind of ledge in the rock up there. If we could just get up to it, that would at least give us a little more time.'

'Well, let's try!' said George. 'The rock wall's nothing like so wet here. We ought to be able to climb it more easily.'

There was one problem, though – how were they to haul Timmy up? The poor dog couldn't climb rocks! Dick soon thought of something. He always had a whole collection of assorted objects in his pockets – penknives, pencils and so on – and now he produced a piece of thin but strong string. He tied one end to Timmy's collar.

'Once we're up we can pull him after us,' he said.

'You'll strangle him!' protested George.

'No, it'll be very fast – he won't have time to

strangle. I don't suppose he'll like it, but you want to save his life, don't you?'

The water was still rising. Anne and the boys began to climb, all helping each other over the difficult bits, and soon they reached the safety of the ledge. George had stayed down below with Timmy, so that she could lift him as high as possible when Dick hauled on the string.

'Good, brave dog!' she told him, when the moment came. 'It won't take long, I promise. Right – haul away, Dick!'

A split second later, a rather indignant Timmy was up on the ledge too. George, who was nimble as a monkey, soon joined the others.

The Five sat there, backs to the wall, watching the waves down below them. 'How – how long do you think it will take to reach us?' asked Anne in a very small voice.

'Oh, it may not rise this far at all,' said Julian, who wanted to comfort his little sister.

George and Dick looked up, wondering if they might be able to climb even higher. They had forgotten all about the treasure now – all they thought of was their own safety.

All of a sudden, as she shifted slightly on the narrow ledge, George slipped and almost fell. Automatically, she grabbed a spur of rock which was jutting out just within her reach. And to the astonishment of them all, the rocky spur moved. They heard a strange noise – and a whole slab of rock swung aside, pivoting on its own axis, to reveal a cavity shaped like a doorway, with a dark hole above it.

Once the children had got over their surprise, they wondered what on earth this meant. Could it be possible that their safety *and* the treasure itself lay at the end of this new passage? What should they do now?

'Go down it!' said Dick. 'The water's still rising!'

'Hang on a minute,' said Julian. 'First we have to make sure we can manoeuvre the slab of rock from inside the tunnel.'

So Dick went into the tunnel on his own. He groped about for a bit, and then found a jutting stone which enabled him to close the opening again. Next he opened it once more, and cheerfully beckoned the others to join him. He closed the 'door' again after them.

'Come on, then!' he said.

'I say, have you noticed something?' said George, a minute or so later. 'Not only can we walk along this tunnel quite easily, but it's nothing like so dark in here.'

'I think that's because of the phosphorescent lichen on the walls,' said Julian. 'Mind where you put your feet, Anne – watch out for loose stones.'

But it really was quite easy to walk down the tunnel. Quite soon the Five came out in a second cave. The whole of this one was underground, but daylight came in through slanting cracks in the rocky ceiling. These cracks were narrow, and Julian guessed that they were probably almost invisible from the outside.

The floor of this cave, unlike the one by the sea, was perfectly flat and, to their amazement and delight, the children saw a big chest with iron bands round it standing there, right in the middle of the cave.

'The picture-writing!' breathed George. 'There's the chest – and the straight line meant a flat floor! Now we've decoded the whole message!'

'*And* found the treasure!' cried Dick joyfully. 'It must be in the chest, mustn't it?'

The children could hardly believe their luck. Almost timidly, they went up to the chest. It was rusty-looking, but still an impressive sight. They felt sure it contained the treasure which the Templars had given into the safekeeping of Sir Hubert de Monksmoor.

'Let's open it!' said Anne.

The iron bands were so rusty that they soon gave way as the children worked to get the chest open – and once they had lifted the lid, what a sight they saw!

'Isn't it lovely?' cried Anne, delighted.

And it was! The four children gazed at the contents of the chest: gold and silver coins, sparkling precious stones of all colours, gold plate, finely worked gold and silver ornaments, mirrors set with gems, beautiful pieces of jewellery. They couldn't

take their dazzled eyes off the chest.

'Well – so we've found the treasure after all!' said Julian, with some awe.

And suddenly they exploded with delight! All the children started jumping about, singing and dancing, while the excited Timmy jumped around too, barking loudly.

'Mr Lofting will be rich!'

'Won't Veronica and Terence be pleased!'

'And won't Mr Long and Mr Short be cross!'

When they had all calmed down a bit, Julian brought them down to earth, and the practical question of what to do next. 'I suppose we'll just have to wait here until the tide goes down and we can get along the beach path again,' he said.

'Never mind. We can pass the time seeing just what's in this treasure chest,' said George.

'Oh dear!' sighed Anne, 'Aunt Fanny and Uncle Quentin will be dreadfully worried about us. We've been gone ages – they must be searching everywhere.'

'Well, there's nothing we can do about that,' said Dick, philosophically, 'so let's just settle down to wait.'

At long last the children worked out that the tide must have gone down. They carefully closed the entrance to the hiding place of the treasure, and clambered down to the beach again. The storm had blown itself out long ago. It was quite late in the afternoon now, and though the children were feeling terribly tired, they bravely set off to walk home. They followed the path along the foot of the cliffs for some way, and then they saw a group of people in the distance, clustered around a boat.

'My word!' said George, who had very sharp eyes. 'That looks like my rowing boat!'

The children began to run. As they came closer to the group, they recognised the tall figure of Uncle Quentin. He was talking to a frogman, and the Sergeant from Kirrin police station was there too, along with a couple of his police constables.

'Father! Father!' shouted George. 'Here we are!'

Uncle Quentin turned and saw the Five. He went quite pale, and then quite red in the face, and held out his arms! All the children rushed towards him.

'Good heavens, children, how glad I am to see you!' said the usually rather forbidding Uncle Quentin. 'You seemed to have disappeared, and we thought you must be drowned, because George's boat was found empty and drifting. Everyone's been out searching!'

'And we're very glad to see you safe and sound, too!' said the Sergeant, beaming. 'Where on earth have you young people been?'

Instead of replying, George went to her boat, and picked up the end of rope which was still tied to its bows. It was a stout, orange, nylon rope. She looked at it hard.

'See that?' she said to her father and the Sergeant. 'I don't expect you've noticed, but this rope's been cut, or rather somebody's sawn through it with a knife. Someone who knew we were well out of the way inside a cave, and wanted to make sure we didn't have a boat to get us home!'

'Now, whatever's all this, young George?' said the Sergeant, rather sternly. 'What a tale to invent! Nobody would think of playing such a trick on you!'

'Oh, wouldn't they just!' said Dick. 'We know two people who jolly well would. They're Mr Foster and Mr Lawson, who are lodgers at Monksmoor Farmhouse.'

'But – but *why*?' asked Uncle Quentin.

'Because we were all hunting for the treasure of the Templars,' George explained, 'and they wanted to keep us from finding it first.'

'Why, there's no such thing as that there treasure!' said one of the policemen, disbelievingly. 'That's just an old tale!'

'No, honestly it isn't!' said Anne in her gentle little voice. 'It really does exist, and what's more we've found it, so that proves it!'

And as the grown-ups all exclaimed with amazement, the children told the tale of their extraordinary adventure – though they had to cut it rather short, because Uncle Quentin was urging them into his car.

'We must hurry home and set your mother's

mind at rest, George,' he said. 'Sergeant, would you and your men follow us? I think we ought to clear all this up.'

Soon the children were back at Kirrin Cottage. Aunt Fanny was overjoyed to see them home safe and sound. She had been dreadfully worried! The children felt much better once they had had a hot bath, and put on clean, dry clothes, and were sitting down to a good tea. As they tucked into a huge pile of hot buttered toast, they told their story in detail.

'Well, children,' said the Sergeant, 'you'll have to take us to this hiding place you've found. That chest is treasure-trove, and we'll have to take it into custody while we go through the formalities of establishing who gets it. I dare say it'll be divided between the owner of the land where it was discovered, and you as the finders.'

'Oh, Mr Lofting owns the land!' said Julian at once. 'The treasure's buried underneath his fields – he owns all the land between his farmhouse and the cliffs on that part of the coast.'

'And there's something else urgent to be done,' said George. 'Sergeant, you must arrest Mr Long and Mr Sh – I mean Mr Foster and Mr Lawson! They're not to be trusted!'

'No,' said Dick. 'They deserve punishing!'

The Sergeant scratched his head. 'Well, I don't know about that!' he said. 'From what you say, you can't *prove* anything against these two gentlemen!'

'You could question them, though,' said Anne, sounding unusually firm.

'Well, why not?' said the Sergeant, smiling at the little girl. 'Answering a few questions won't do them any harm. I'll say I need to check someone's identity – that's it! Yes. I'll be off to Monskmoor Farmhouse straight away.'

'Can we come with you?' asked Julian.

'Well . . . well, I can't exactly forbid you to go along at the same time as we do, can I?' said the Sergeant, with a grin. 'Seeing as your own young friends live there!'

Uncle Quentin too thought he would like to meet these two treasure-hunting rivals of the Five, so he took the children in his car, and they followed the police car to the farmhouse.

Just as they arrived, Foster and Lawson were coming out of the house. At the sight of the policemen, the two men looked round in some alarm. That rather intrigued the Sergeant, who asked if they had anything on them that proved their identity, such as a driving licence or an official letter.

'Er – well – ' said Mr Lawson, otherwise Mr Short. 'Well, not actually *on* us, but I'll go and find you something.'

And the two men turned to hurry off. But Timmy wasn't having any of that!

By now he thoroughly disliked the pair of them – not only had they thrown him that poisoned meatball, but they had hit him hard when he tried to defend George's boat. He wanted to leap at them. Privately, George thought that was quite a good idea, but she had to hold him back. Suddenly, however, he broke away from her and made a dash for 'Mr Long', the big, tall man.

He *was* a tall man, however, and Timmy, going for his throat, missed and closed his jaws on the chest pocket of the man's denim jacket. His teeth tore the material – and a whole sheaf of papers fell out at the Sergeant's feet. The Sergeant bent to pick them up. One glance at them, and he gave a sign to the constables, who moved in on the two men.

'Well, well, well!' said the Sergeant. 'So you thought you'd just walk away, eh? It strikes me your consciences aren't exactly clear! And you claim to be called Foster – well, there's plenty of stuff here showing that's not your real name at all. Let's see about your friend.'

He put out his hand, and one of the policemen passed him some papers which he had just taken out of the little dark man's pocket.

'Aha!' said the Sergeant. 'So you're going under a false name too? And what's more, both your real names came up on the list of wanted men circulated only the other day to every police force in this part of the country. I think you've got some explaining to do! Off to the cells with you for the time being!'

'I knew there was something fishy about them!'

said Dick.

'Dangerous, too,' said George. 'It's no thanks to them we're still alive to show you where the treasure is!' And she said exactly what she thought the two men had done.

'That little girl's out of her mind!' said 'Mr Short', pretending to be very indignant. 'What – us unhook her anchor and chain? What nonsense! We've never even set eyes on this picture-writing she mentions.'

'Oh no?' said the Sergeant, looking at one of the pieces of paper he had picked up. 'Then how do I come to find a copy of it falling out of your pocket?'

'Well, we certainly had nothing to do with setting that rowing boat adrift,' said the dark little man – but it soon became obvious that this was another lie. Timmy, straining at his leash, managed to get away from George again. Seeing the dog run at him, the dark man took a knife from his pocket and flicked it open.

'If that dog comes any closer, I'll kill him!' he shouted.

'Stop, Timmy – heel!' cried George, only just in time. Timmy obeyed her at once. And then she let out a cry of triumph.

She had just seen something.

'Look at his knife, Sergeant – oh, do take a good look at it!' she said. The Sergeant took the man's knife from him. 'There – look!' George repeated. 'Its blade folds up, and do you see that bit of orange nylon thread caught in it? That came from the rope attached to my anchor. So that *proves* he cut it!'

It was obvious now that the two men's game was up, and the police took them away to ask them some more questions.

Meanwhile, another policeman had called on the Loftings, who could hardly believe their good fortune. The children told the Sergeant that even if any of the treasure-trove belonged to them, they didn't want it – they wanted all of it to go to the Loftings, so that the hard-working farmer could pay back the money he owed, and Mrs Lofting needn't serve cream teas any more. Though secretly, the Five rather hoped she wouldn't give that up! Veronica and Terence were delighted.

Then they all went back to Kirrin Cottage to celebrate. Aunt Fanny was very pleased to hear that the end of the treasure hunt had turned out so well, and gave all the children a hug.

'And do you know the funniest thing of all, Mother?' George asked her. 'You remember we called those two men Mr Long and Mr Short, because of their different heights? Well, one of them really *is* called Long!'

'And it's the short one!' said Dick, laughing.

If you have enjoyed this book you may like to read some more exciting adventures from Knight Books. Here is a complete list of Enid Blyton's FAMOUS FIVE adventures:

1. Five on a Treasure Island
2. Five go Adventuring Again
3. Five Run Away Together
4. Five go to Smuggler's Top
5. Five go off in a Caravan
6. Five on Kirrin Island Again
7. Five go off to Camp
8. Five get into Trouble
9. Five fall into Adventure
10. Five on a Hike Together
11. Five have a Wonderful Time
12. Five go down to the Sea
13. Five go to Mystery Moor
14. Five have Plenty of Fun
15. Five on a Secret Trail
16. Five go to Billycock Hill
17. Five get into a Fix
18. Five on Finniston Farm
19. Five go to Demon's Rocks
20. Five have a Mystery to Solve
21. Five are Together Again

WILLARD PRICE

A complete list of his thrilling animal adventures:

1. Amazon Adventure
2. South Sea Adventure
3. Underwater Adventure
4. Volcano Adventure
5. Whale Adventure
6. African Adventure
7. Elephant Adventure
8. Safari Adventure
9. Lion Adventure
10. Gorilla Adventure
11. Diving Adventure
12. Cannibal Adventure
13. Tiger Adventure
14. Arctic Adventure

Hal and Roger Hunt are sent all over the world by their father in search of rare animals with which to supply zoos. Their adventures on the way are full of action and suspense and every book is packed with information about the remoter regions of the earth, together with encyclopaedic facts about the world's animal kingdom.

KNIGHT BOOKS